THE MOST FAMOUS ILLEGAL GOOSE CREEK PARADE

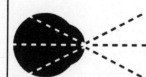

This Large Print Book carries the
Seal of Approval of N.A.V.H.

THE MOST FAMOUS ILLEGAL GOOSE CREEK PARADE

VIRGINIA SMITH

THORNDIKE PRESS
A part of Gale, Cengage Learning

GALE
CENGAGE Learning·

Farmington Hills, Mich • San Francisco • New York • Waterville, Maine
Meriden, Conn • Mason, Ohio • Chicago

GALE
CENGAGE Learning®

LIBRARY OF CONGRESS CATALOGING-IN-PUBLICATION DATA

Smith, Virginia, 1960–
    The most famous illegal Goose Creek parade / by Virginia Smith. — Large print edition.
        pages cm. — (Thorndike Press large print Christian fiction) (Tales from the Goose Creek B&B #1)
    ISBN 978-1-4104-8492-5 (hardcover) — ISBN 1-4104-8492-0 (hardcover)
    1. City and town life—Kentucy—Fiction. 2. Bed and breakfast accommodations—Fiction. 3. Large type books. I. Title.
PS3619.M5956M67 2016
813'.6—dc23   2015031721

Published in 2016 by arrangement with Harvest House Publishers

Printed in Mexico
1 2 3 4 5 6 7 19 18 17 16

THE MOST FAMOUS ILLEGAL GOOSE CREEK PARADE

CHAPTER ONE

"Oh, Albert, isn't it lovely?"

Al tore his gaze from the towering monstrosity before him to cast a disbelieving stare at his wife. Hands folded beneath her chin as if in rapturous prayer, Millie's eyes sparkled. She gazed at the house as if she'd just caught sight of Buckingham Palace. He glanced back at the colossal three-story structure looming on the horizon across a stretch of neglected lawn the size of a football field. In fact, the house did have a castle-like look about it, with that round tower spiraling upward from a disturbingly asymmetrical roof.

The weather had finally turned mild after a brutal Kentucky winter, and they'd been able to resume the pleasant habit of an evening stroll after supper. The slight breeze that ruffled Al's hair — he must remember to stop by Fred's for a trim this weekend — still held a chill, but nothing like the icy blasts that had persisted all the way through the second week of March. Al preferred their regular route, which took them down Goose Creek's picturesque Main Street, but tonight Millie had wanted to walk through the town's oldest neighborhood to see if she could spot any blossoming jonquils. They spied sprouts aplenty, clusters of narrow green leaves with slender stalks straining skyward to catch the last rays of evening sunlight, but the blossoms were still tightly cocooned within their protective wrappings. Kind of like Al. He huddled deeper within the collar of his heavy jacket and looked again at the house.

Millie seemed to be waiting, so he ventured an answer. "It's the old Updyke place."

A completely unenlightened comment, but a cautious one. Thirty-six years of marriage had taught him a few things. Until he uncovered the reason for that gleam in his wife's eye, the wisest course was to stick with stating the obvious.

She ignored him, as she was apt to do when concocting an idea in that brain of hers. "Look at the gables, all those charming levels of the roof. And the chimneys. And that bay window! It's absolutely gorgeous."

8

He cocked his head to change his angle of inspection. Under no definition of the word would he call a broken, boarded-up window *gorgeous*. "Be expensive to replace that curved glass. Probably a special order."

"And you know there's a verandah in the back. It overlooks the lake."

The faint sound of alarms began clanging in the recesses of Al's brain. Surely this conversation wasn't headed where he feared. "It's not a lake, it's a pond. Probably covered in scum. Water draws skeeters," he cautioned. "And gnats."

She dismissed his warning by waving a set of pink manicured fingernails in his direction. "That's what screens are for. That verandah could be screened in easily, and think how peaceful it would be to look at the water over coffee in the mornings. I'll bet there are geese or ducks or something. We could be like Katharine Hepburn and Henry Fonda in *On Golden Pond*."

The volume of the alarms rose in his inner ears. Now she was imagining herself in that disaster of a house. Al didn't like the way this conversation was going, not one bit. "Those shingles are in bad shape. Bet they leak. Probably water damage inside. I can't even imagine how much it would cost to put a roof on that place."

A faint nod in answer told him she was barely listening. He added a note of sternness to his tone.

"And I'd be afraid to step onto that porch. Looks like it might collapse. No telling what shape the rest of the house is in after sitting empty for so long. Must be ten years since the Updykes left."

"What a silly thing to say. It's perfectly safe."

"How can you be sure? Nobody's been in that place in a decade."

"Of course they have. Louise Gaitskill says the interior is in wonderful shape considering the house is over a hundred years old."

The ringing in his ears became a claxon. Louise Gaitskill was not one of Millie's circle of friends. To his knowledge they didn't know each other well enough to enter into a casual chat about a deserted Victorian eyesore like this house. But a professional conversation?

Louise Gaitskill was a realtor.

He whirled to study his wife head-on through narrowed lids. "What are you getting at, Mildred Richardson? Out with it."

A wistful smile twitched at the corners of her lips. "Only that I've loved this house since I was a girl. I went to a birthday party there once. We ate cupcakes out on the verandah and played croquet." A quiet sigh escaped her lips. "I used to wonder what it was like to be rich and live in an elegant house like this one." She did not meet his eye but continued to stare at the house. "And I happened to hear that the Updyke brothers have finally agreed to sell it."

Aha! The truth emerged at last. Well, he'd better put the skids on this conversation right now. "We are *not* buying that house. Under no circumstances. Not even the slightest possibility. I refuse to discuss it, so put the idea out of your head."

To prevent the inevitable argument he stalked away from her in the direction of the perfectly good home where they'd lived happily for nearly two decades, using his long-legged stride to its full advantage.

Quick footsteps scuffed on the road as she hurried to catch up. "But Louise says they told her they're desperate for money and need to sell quickly. She thinks they'd be willing to let it go at a fraction of its value."

"Louise is not a very good realtor if she tells people her clients are desperate." He stared straight ahead, not slowing one smidge even though she had to trot in order to keep up with him.

"But they want her to," Millie argued. "They don't care if everyone knows, because they want to unload —" She bit off the rest of the sentence.

Al pounced on the word with glee. "They want to *unload* a potential real estate catastrophe before the house collapses."

"No," she said as calmly as she could while huffing with the effort of staying beside him. "They need the money to renovate the restaurant they bought up in Cincinnati before the building inspector shuts them down."

From the corner of his eye he spied a flush splotching her cheeks. Guilt pricked his conscience, and he shortened his stride. "They had no business opening that restaurant to begin with."

"Oh, don't be an old poop." She gave his arm a playful nudge and settled into the slower pace. "It was their dream. Everybody should follow their dream if they have the chance."

A longing glance over her shoulder was no doubt designed to inflict the maximum guilt on the "old poop" who dashed her girlish dreams of living in a grand house. Well, he refused to succumb to her obvious machinations. He loved this woman intensely, so much that in quiet times of reflection he could scarcely breathe at the depth of his feelings, but he was not blind to her ways. Over the years he'd fallen victim to her womanly wiles more than once. That's how they'd ended up with two sets of golf clubs collecting dust in the attic and a bright pink Volkswagen Beetle with obnoxious curling eyelashes over the headlights. And Rufus, the world's smelliest beagle. Not to mention a third child, though Allison was a joy he'd never regretted for an instant.

He shook off the tenderness that always accompanied thoughts of his only daughter. Now was not the time for softness. Millie could sense the slightest shift in his mood and would not hesitate to press the advantage with a ruthlessness at odds to her sweet manner and delightful dimples.

"We are not buying that house." He punctuated the statement with a firm shake of his head.

His proclamation was met with silence. Al risked a sideways glance, and was not comforted by what he saw. A smile, nearly imperceptible and composed of unbendable steel, hovered about the lovely full lips. He knew that expression well, and the sight of it set his insides to quivering. She had no intention of giving in. And the truth that he had come to realize over the years, the one he tried to hide from her at all costs, was that in a match of wills, hers was the stronger.

Millie held her tongue for the duration of their stroll. Aware of the cautious glances Albert shot her way every so often, she maintained a pleasant expression. Pouting, she'd learned long ago, would serve no purpose besides irritating her peace-loving husband. When Albert was irritated, he became even more mule-headed than usual. At this stage of the negotiations it was extremely important to keep every conversation cordial.

She knew how his mind worked. He would process their discussion over the next few days. At odd times he would utter an objection out of the blue. While buttering his toast he might say, "That lawn is a disaster, you know." Or when he slid into bed at night, "The property taxes are probably triple what we pay now." She would reply with a smile and a nod and revel in a secret satisfaction. Let him brood over the downsides, all the while becoming accustomed to the idea.

Turning the corner onto Mulberry Avenue, she eyed the familiar street with fresh eyes. Blacktopped driveways and arrow-straight sidewalks outlined squares of neatly maintained lawns, identical in size. Single-story homes of similar size and construction, though with enough individuality to give the neighborhood a pleasant, non-tract-like feel. Her gaze was drawn to their house in the exact center of the street. The holly bushes on either side of their mailbox, though winter-dull at the moment, were trimmed to perfect roundness. A row of carefully tended Camellia shrubs, equally spaced in a strip of dark soil lining the sidewalk, led to the front door. At the moment they were mere bundles of sticks but had recently begun to show signs of producing the glossy dark leaves and pink blossoms that would lend an air of glory to the Richardson yard that none of their neighbors had managed to replicate. Thanks to Albert.

She cast a fond glance sideways, ignoring the stubborn set to his strong jaw. Such a perfectionist. It was one of the traits she admired about him. He approached every task with a thoroughness and determination that sometimes bordered on compulsiveness, and he never left a job half-done. He might grumble but she knew he loved the work, derived immense satisfaction from tackling new projects. The sight of a broken toilet handle or a chip in the wall paint rendered him positively gleeful. Without a doubt, his efforts to landscape their yard saved him from suffering a stroke after that alarming episode three summers ago. She herself had seen his blood pressure retreat to the normal range whenever he plunged his hands into rich Kentucky soil.

But now all the chores were done, inside the house and out. Retirement was only a few years away, and then what? Their home was in perfect repair.

Ah, but the Updyke property had *plenty* to do. Years' worth of projects to keep them both busy and healthy.

When they approached Violet's house, the curtains in the front window moved. Her best friend and next-door neighbor for nearly twenty years stood inside, peering at them through the binoculars she kept in readiness on the hall table. Probably beside herself with waiting to see how the conversation with Albert went. With a cautious glance at her husband, Millie gave a very slight shake of her head. The curtains fell back into place.

They stepped from the sidewalk onto their walkway, and Albert's face lost the perturbed expression. She spied the beginnings of a smile as he scanned the neat lawn, the gleaming windows, the front door he'd painted an inviting shade of red. Yes, their home was pleasant and welcoming, and in excellent shape. According to Louise Gaitskill, it would bring a good price.

She allowed him to open the door for her and let her hand linger on his cheek with a gentle caress as she passed inside. After all these years of marriage, you'd think Albert would learn that she always had his best interests in mind.

CHAPTER TWO

"Oh, just the usual complaints," the old veterinarian assured Susan. "You know. Ear mites. Hookworm. Acute moist dermatitis. UTDs in the cats, of course. And fleas are bad around here. Standard stuff. Nothing you can't handle."

Susan worried the inside of her cheek between her molars. His vote of confidence in her skills meant absolutely zero since he'd only met her an hour before. How did he know what she, a brand new veterinarian with the ink barely dry on her license, could handle? On the other hand, she was certainly competent to diagnose and treat the common health problems of household pets. If he were telling the truth about his clientele, she shouldn't have any problems taking over his practice.

If he were telling the truth. The suspicious thought snagged in her mental filter and dangled there at the front of her mind.

What's the matter with me? He seems like an honest man. There's no reason at all to suspect Dr. Forsythe of being untruthful.

No reason beyond her habitual mistrust of strangers and the certainty that all men except Daddy were out to take advantage of a female undertaking a business transaction alone in order to soak them for as much as they could. Which was ridiculous. This was a reputable doctor of veterinary medicine retiring from his practice, not someone trying to sell her a timeshare.

They stood behind a low counter in the otherwise empty reception area, their conversation accompanied by cries for attention from a Yorkie and a Chow mix in the boarding room down the hall. The poor dogs had been excited to see them during her after-hours tour of the facility, and clearly expected to be let out of their kennels for a play period. The odors of disinfectant and pine lingered in the air and overpowered the more common smells that accompanied a vet's office, proof that the floors had been recently mopped.

"Will you be available for consultations if the *new doctor* has questions?" She emphasized the words in a clear message that she had not yet made a decision to sign the papers and become that new doctor.

"By phone, of course." His pleasant expression did not fade in the least. "But the missus and I are moving to Florida as soon as we wrap things up here."

She nodded, scanning the reception counter. A dog cookie jar sat on one end, and a kitty treat jar on the other. From this vantage point she could see into both of the small waiting rooms, four blue plastic chairs situated in each. A sign suspended from the ceiling in front of a partition between the two directed *Playful Pups* to the left and *Kuddly Kitties* to the right.

Where did Disagreeable Dogs and Cantankerous Cats wait?

Dismissing the snarky thought, she asked, "What about reptiles? Do you treat many of those?"

Though most of her vet school classmates avoided caring for reptiles if they could, Susan loved them. She shared her apartment with a bearded dragon she had inherited during a practicum when he escaped the confines of an inadequate enclosure and surprised his owner's mother in the shower. The stunt, apparently the last of many, had resulted in banishment from the family home. Susan had assured the tearful little boy that she would take good care of Puff and love him forever.

Susan never broke a promise.

"Not many," the doctor admitted. "I'm afraid things are pretty common in Goose Creek. Very few exotics. Nothing out of the ordinary to speak of." His expression brightened with a sudden memory. "Though Clete Watson's boa constrictor did come down with a skin fungus last year."

"You treated it with Canesten cream?"

"Yup. Cleared up in a couple of days." The man's lips curved into a broad smile. "You know your stuff. I had to look up the treatment. Makes me feel better, knowing I'm leaving my patients in competent hands."

Now he was flattering her, something to which Susan was not susceptible in the least. *If* she decided to buy the Goose Creek Animal Clinic from Dr. Forsythe, the decision would be based on a careful analysis of all available facts. And in order to thoroughly analyze the situation and make an informed business decision, there was one more thing she must do.

"I'll want to inspect your records," she told him. "Accounting, payroll, and of course the patient charts."

"I thought you would. It's all in here." He patted the top of the computer monitor on the reception desk. "My receptionist convinced me to convert from paper last year.

Against my will, I might add, but I figured I'd better get automated before I handed the place over to someone else. A young person like you probably knows your way around a computer better than your own living room, but an old man like me needs things written out." He picked up a thin folder from the desk and extended it toward her. "The password and instructions are here. Have at it."

Startled, she stared at the folder without taking it. "You mean now?"

He tossed a set of keys on the desk. "You drove all the way up here to see the place, so there's no time like the present. I'm going to take those pups out for a romp before I head home for the night. You'll lock up, won't you?"

He was going to leave her here alone? Was he insane? How did he know she was trustworthy?

Shock must have shown on her face, because he gave her an encouraging smile. "After you contacted me last week I called a couple of your professors, longtime friends of mine. They vouched for you." He winked. "And besides, the petty cash and all the good drugs are locked in the safe." With a final grin he set the folder on the desk and disappeared behind the door leading to the clinic section. A moment later the dogs' plaintive yips changed to joyful barks and she heard the clang of kennel doors being opened.

Susan hesitated only a moment before seating herself in the rolling chair. She reached for the folder, a sense of excitement swelling inside her chest. If the books looked as good as she expected, she was going to do it. Take Daddy up on his offer to cosign a loan, buy a veterinary clinic, break her apartment lease, and move to Goose Creek, Kentucky.

Heaven help her.

The evening wore on with Millie maintaining a pleasant attitude that nagged at Al. What scheme was she cooking up? He found it impossible to concentrate on *Wheel of Fortune* and *Jeopardy* with her sitting there, rocking and knitting and humming an off-key tune like she hadn't a care in the world. Even his favorite show, *Person of Interest,* failed to distract him. How could it with that gargantuan house lurking in his mind like a monster, overshadowing his thoughts?

Over a hundred years old, she'd said. Probably hadn't been maintained at all. Old man Updyke had been a pinchfist.

He aimed a scowl in her direction. "I'll bet the plumbing is original."

She looked up from her knitting, eyebrows arched over inquisitive eyes. "What was that, dear?"

"The Updyke place. Like as not those old pipes are et up with corrosion. Wiring's probably shot too. That place is nothing more than a giant tinderbox. One spark and *poof.*" He sketched an explosion in the air with his hands.

"Ah." Her head dipped serenely before she returned to her task.

Al glowered as he directed his attention to the fifty-two-inch flat screen television the kids had given him for Christmas. He couldn't see a thing beyond the image of that steeply pitched roof, the shingles ruffled like a frilly bedspread. No repairing that mess. They'd have to put on an entire new roof, and all those steep levels and chimneys would cost a fortune.

From his bed between their chairs Rufus gave a quiet yip in his sleep and his back legs buffeted the air. Squirrel-chasing dreams, no doubt. It was the dog's single redeeming grace, as far as Al could see. Rufus hated squirrels with a passion and successfully kept their yard and birdfeeders squirrel-free. Of course he'd been known to tear through screen doors when he spied one, and once the pursuit of his mission had cost them a set of living room draperies.

There were probably hundreds of squirrels living in all those massive trees surrounding the Updyke house. Maybe thousands.

Millie's cheerful voice interrupted his brooding. "How about a slice of lemon cake?"

"What?" Al twisted in his chair to level a wide-eyed stare on her. Lemon cake, made from his dear mother's recipe, was his favorite dessert in the world. A staple at family Christmas and Easter celebrations, the recipe called for the cake to sit for three days entombed in a cocoon of plastic wrap in order for the tangy glaze to fully saturate every spongy morsel.

Was there no end to the woman's machinations? No depth to which she would not sink?

"Lemon cake," she repeated, wrapping her knitting needles in yet another half-finished wooly scarf and stowing the bundle in the basket at her side. "I made it on Wednesday."

On Wednesday? So this scheme wasn't a spur-of-the-moment idea at all. She had two days' head start on him.

He allowed suspicion to saturate his tone. "Why?"

Her eyes widened. "For tomorrow, of course. But you seem out of sorts this evening, so I thought a treat might put you in a better mood. I think two days is long enough, just this once."

Tomorrow? Tomorrow was Saturday. Nothing special about a Saturday besides being a weekend. Saturdays did not warrant lemon cake in and of themselves. Something else then. Were the kids coming for the weekend? Lord, he hoped not. He loved them dearly, of course, but baby Lionel was a handful now that he'd started to walk. A glance around the room revealed that Millie had not put her immense collection of knickknacks up out of the toddler's range. Not the kids then.

Wait. What was the date? This morning he'd turned the page on his calendar to March twenty-third. So tomorrow was the twenty-fourth.

Drat!

He'd forgotten their anniversary.

"A piece of cake would be good," he conceded with a nod.

Millie bustled out of the room, humming. Rufus bounded to his feet mid-snore and waddled after her, no doubt hoping for a handout.

Al stared after them, chagrinned at his lapse. No need to admit his near-error. He'd get up early and run out for a card. Maybe pick up some flowers too, something special in light of the lemon cake. After thirty-six years of marriage — no, thirty-seven — they'd moved beyond the gift stage decades ago. He settled deeper in his recliner, his taste buds anticipating the first delicious bite of sugary tartness.

Then he jolted straight up as realization struck him like a slap in the face. Millie did know him well. His mood was lighter already. That in itself was more than a little alarming.

Millie sat in bed, leaning against fluffy pillows and paging through the *Better Homes and Gardens* she'd picked up at the Save-A-Lot that morning. This month was a special issue devoted entirely to old home renovations, which she and Violet agreed must be the Lord giving a divine nod to her plans for the Updyke house. So many beautiful pictures of country kitchens, updated bathrooms, and cozy bedrooms. Already the image of the entry hall she would create loomed clearly in her mind's eye. Comfortable and welcoming, something that would set people at ease the moment they stepped through the doorway. Not too much furniture, or it would feel crowded. A simple runner on the floor, a few old-fashiony pictures on the walls. A small table, a coat rack, and maybe an antique wooden bench. She'd always admired those. The handrail on the stairway would take on a regal gleam with a little polish and a lot of work.

When Albert came out of the bathroom in his pajamas, she casually set the magazine face-down on her nightstand.

"That yard is mammoth," he announced as he slid beneath the comforter beside her. "Do you know how long it would take to mow it?" He pounded his pillow, a tad more violently than necessary, and settled his head into the indentation.

"You could buy a riding mower." The moment the suggestion left her mouth, she realized her mistake.

Albert sat straight up. "Do you know how much those things cost?" Accusation sparked in the glare he turned on her. "I'm not made of money, you know. I'm retiring in three years. *Three years,* Millie. We need to start tightening our belts. Saving our pennies. Stretching every dime."

"You sound like Violet," she remarked mildly.

Momentarily distracted, his mouth snapped shut. Violet's constant use of clichés drove her husband insane.

"In this case, it's justified. Mildred Richardson, you've gotten an idea in that head of yours and it's addled your brains. You're not thinking clearly. We need to be on the same page, now more than ever." He warmed visibly to his topic. "Retirement looms, Millie. It looms over us like clouds on the horizon. Those clouds can be white and fluffy" — the heavy creases on his brow deepened — "or they can be dark and threatening."

Oh, dear. His voice had taken on the dramatic tone of a bad Shakespearian actor. Never a good sign.

"Don't take on so, dear. Remember your blood pressure."

"I *am* remembering my blood pressure," he countered. "What do you think my blood pressure will be when I'm seventy-two years old and forced to go back to work because we've spent all our money fixing that behemoth of a house? By then the computer industry will have left me behind. My skills will be obsolete." Reproach settled over his features. "I'll have to go to work as a

Walmart greeter. Is that what you want, Millie?"

"Now you're just being ridiculous." She rearranged her pillow. "You act as if the house were ready to collapse, and you haven't even seen it. For all you know it might be in perfect condition. It could be a real bargain. Maybe even an opportunity to *make* money."

There. Though that was definitely a broad hint at step two in her plan, it wouldn't hurt to let him ponder the idea of making money. She turned off the light on her nightstand and slid lower beneath the comforter. "The least you could do is look at the house so we know what we're turning down."

In the silence that followed, she turned onto her side — facing Albert, because after all tomorrow was their anniversary and she did love him and didn't want him to think she was angry with him even though he was being stubborn — and closed her eyes in preparation for sleep.

"Fine. I'll look at it."

Surprised, Millie's eyes flew open. "You will?"

"As an anniversary present." His expression hardened. "And just so you know, while we're inspecting the house I intend to point out all the flaws and pitfalls of this crazy

30

scheme so you will put it out of your mind once and for all."

Of course he would. But getting him through the door was an important step, and it had happened rather more easily than she'd expected. An excellent sign.

"I would expect nothing less." Millie sat up to place a tender kiss on her husband's tight lips and felt them soften beneath hers. "Thank you. I love you."

"Do you?" His eyes searched hers. "Even after thirty-seven years?"

"Now more than ever." She flashed one of the dimples he loved to kiss. "Turn off that light and I'll prove it."

With a click darkness descended, and Millie nestled into the familiar warm embrace of her husband's arms.

MOTHER RICHARDSON'S
LEMON CAKE

Cake

3/4 cup oil

1 cup canned apricot nectar (comes in a can in the juice section)

4 eggs

1/2 cup sugar

1 lemon cake mix

Glaze

1 1/2 cups confectioners' sugar

1/4 cup lemon juice

Preheat oven to 350 degrees. Grease and flour a Bundt cake pan. Mix all ingredients thoroughly and pour into prepared pan. Bake at 350 for 25 minutes, then reduce the temperature to 325 and bake for another 25 minutes. Cool slightly, then remove cake and turn it over onto a cake stand or cake carrier with a cover. While the cake is still hot, poke all over with a toothpick, and then pour on the glaze.

Cover the cake stand, and then wrap the covered stand tightly with several layers of plastic wrap. Let the cake sit for 2 to 3 days before serving.

CHAPTER THREE

Ah, Saturday! Al stood on the back deck gazing out over his orderly lawn and lifted his coffee mug in a salute to the day. In just over three years he would join the ranks of the retired, and every day would be Saturday.

Except Sundays, of course. Retirement would not alter their Sunday routine. He would still rise at the leisurely hour of seven-thirty, spread the *Herald Leader* across the kitchen table to peruse while he sipped coffee and enjoyed the cozy sound of Millie's humming — hymns on Sundays, of course — while she whipped up a breakfast of their pre-church standard, banana bran muffins and egg white omelets.

And Tuesdays in retirement would not be Saturdays either. The men at Woodview Community Church got together for breakfast on Tuesdays, and he intended to join them once his Tuesdays were free. Oh, and

Thursdays wouldn't be Saturdays either, because —

Mercy! How his thoughts did ramble. He must be getting old.

A movement drew his attention to the corner of the yard. A red-breasted robin fluttered to a landing atop a whitewashed wooden fence-post. Clutched in its beak was a long piece of dried grass. It cocked its head to fix Al with an ebony stare and then launched into the branches of the ornamental crabapple in the center of his yard. Al's spirits rose even higher. The robins returning to the Goose Creek valley, and to his yard, were a welcome sign that spring was truly here.

"Don't worry, Mother Bird," he told the robin in a quiet tone. "I'll hang the feeders soon."

With a glance at a lemon-yellow sun rising into an azure sky, he turned and entered the house.

"I think I'll walk down to Cardwell's and see if anyone's there," he told Millie.

"All right." At the kitchen sink, up to her elbows in soapy water, his wife tilted her cheek for a kiss.

He obliged her and turned to go.

"Why don't you take Rufus with you?"

Al skidded to a halt. He cast a scowl

34

toward the corner where Rufus had stirred enough to raise his head from his cushion at the mention of his name.

"I'm sure he'd much rather stay with you."

Her humming barely paused. "The walk will do him good."

"He doesn't listen to me if you're not there." His voice took on a petulant tone that he abhorred but did nothing to filter. "He adores you. Me, he barely tolerates and then only if you're around to impress."

She flipped on the faucet and rinsed a dish before setting it in the drainer. "Nonsense. Rufus loves you. It's just that you're sterner than I am so he thinks *you* don't like *him*. Try speaking nicely to him."

He deepened his scowl, and the dog's tail gave a cautious wag. With a loud sigh to inform his wife that his capitulation was only for her and not due to any desire to spend time with her pet, Al left the room to retrieve his jacket. He returned with Rufus's leash in hand. Seeing it, the dog leaped off his pillow and began an enthusiastic display of whirling acrobatics, nails tapping an erratic rhythm on the linoleum.

Millie laughed, a delightful sound in any circumstance, and seemed to enjoy watching Al try to snag the animal's collar.

"Hold still, you mutt," he commanded,

and though the dog ignored him he managed to hook a finger beneath the collar and clip the leash in place. Bending at the waist put him in close enough proximity to get a whiff of pungent doggie odor. He wrinkled his nose. "*Phew.* He needs a bath."

"He had one last week. You can't bathe them too often, you know. They'll develop dry skin."

"Hmm."

Rufus headed for the exit, toenails scrabbling as he tugged the leash to its full extent. Al wound his end around his hand and allowed himself to be pulled toward the front door.

"Don't forget your cell phone," Millie called after him. "And turn it on, please."

Cell phones, in his opinion, were a sign of society's downfall. People these days couldn't walk down the street without a phone glued to their ear, inflicting their private conversations on everyone around them and completely inattentive to their surroundings. A plague, that's what they were.

"Why?" he asked. "I'm just going to town. Won't be but an hour or so."

"Because I'm going to call Louise and set up our appointment to see the house. If she can squeeze us in this morning I'll call you."

36

He swallowed a grumble because, after all, he had agreed to inspect the place. A man's word was his word. If only she wouldn't put him in the position of being a naysayer on today, of all days. No doubt she would still be irritated with him over the candlelit anniversary dinner they always enjoyed together.

Even so, he would not temper his opinions, not even in deference to the day. Too much was at stake. It was his duty as a responsible husband to point out the utter foolishness of buying that house at this period in their lives. Being a levelheaded woman who, for the most part, could be persuaded to look at things rationally, Millie was certain to come to the realization that his was the only logical decision.

When the front door closed behind them, Rufus applied himself to his walk with enthusiasm. Straining the leash to its furthest reaches, he dragged Al down the front walk and turned right onto the sidewalk.

"No." Al spoke in the low, firm tone used by the instructor on the dog training video Millie made him watch shortly after she brought Rufus home. "This way."

He tugged, but Rufus ignored him. Grumbling, Al turned left and started walking toward town, his arm extended behind him, muscles tight with the effort of pulling the dog after him. Rufus, sensing the futility of a struggle, changed his mind and his direction. With an energy that belied the hours he spent snoozing on the cushions Millie kept all over the house for him, the dog raced to get ahead of Al. The jolt nearly pulled Al's shoulder out of its socket. The creature took up his position at the extreme length of the leash, panting and straining and occasionally eliciting a choking cough.

Rubbing his shoulder with his free hand, Al glared at the animal. "Just once couldn't you pretend to be a well-behaved canine and walk at my side?"

Apparently not. They continued in that manner to the end of Mulberry Avenue, turned right onto Walnut, and covered the short distance to Main Street at something just shy of a trot, the dog's toenails leaving white scratches on the sidewalk. So much for a leisurely morning stroll.

The collection of two dozen or so mid-1800s buildings that comprised Goose Creek's town proper stretched along either side of a railroad track that ran smack-dab down the center of the street. Some years back the city council had designated that stretch of Main Street one-way on each side of the track, which had created no end of controversy among those who, like Al, resisted any change to the little town they called home. The mayor argued that the change would improve the flow of traffic. The mayor won the argument, but was defeated in the next election and moved to Frankfort to plague that city with improved traffic patterns.

Al allowed himself to be dragged down the raised sidewalk on the south side of the tracks, noting with a mild satisfaction that at least a third of the old buildings boasted For Sale signs in the front windows. Some of his fellow Creekers urged that the town must do something to draw tourism and new residents, or it wouldn't survive. Al unashamedly counted himself one of those who believed that to invite an influx of tourists would spoil the charm of Goose Creek and turn it into a central Kentucky Gatlinburg, a thought that made him shudder.

Cardwell Drugstore, located in the center of Main Street on the northbound side, was a morning gathering place favored by a small group of long-time residents. When first constructed, the building had been a boarding house. Since the decline of the railroad a series of businesses had attempted to claim it, but each ultimately failed. Finally, fifteen years ago, Leonard Cardwell bought it, spent his inheritance repairing the crumbling brick walls and decaying floors, and converted it into an old-fashioned pharmacy. Creekers rewarded his efforts with their wholehearted approval and their patronage. The authentic '50s-style soda fountain quickly became a favorite watering hole. On Saturday mornings the ranks of the regulars swelled with men like Al who made the forty-minute drive to jobs in Lexington during the week.

Al hooked Rufus's leash to one of the lawn jockeys Cardwell had installed on either side of the door for that purpose. Lucy Cardwell obviously anticipated canine visitors this morning, because the buckets had been filled with fresh water. Rufus, panting from exertion, plunged his head into one and slurped noisily.

"Behave yourself," Al told him. The dog ignored him. Naturally.

Bells on the door hanger announced his presence to those already gathered inside. He nodded in response to a half-dozen called greetings. A good turnout this morning. All six stools were occupied so he made his way past the counter to the first of three tables, where Jacob Pulliam sat sipping coffee. He pulled out a spindly-legged chair at the same moment Lucy placed a steaming coffee mug in front of him. Looking up with a smile, he opened his mouth to thank her.

"I heard you're buying the old Updyke house," she said before returning to her perch behind the counter. "Good for you."

His thanks died unuttered. Every head in the room turned while Al's smile melted.

"No kidding?" Jacob leaned across the scarred Formica table. "Mighty pretty, that place. Lotta yard to mow, though."

Pete Lawson, who managed a hardware store in Lexington, twisted on his stool to face them. "And it's gonna need some heavy-duty repair work, too. If 'n you want me to start you a charge account, I c'n do it easy."

Woody Edwards spoke up from beyond Pete. "I got a brother-in-law who does handyman work. I'll give you his number."

The sound of rising blood pressure began a faint buzz in Al's ears. "I am *not* buying the Updyke place."

Lucy's expression became perplexed. "But I just got a text from Betty, who was talking to Sharon Geddes on the phone when she got an e-mail from Louise, and she said you were."

Never underestimate the power of a small town gossip chain fueled by technology.

"I don't care what she said." He spoke a

bit more forcefully than necessary and saw a few eyebrows arch. Swallowing back his rising ire, he went on in a calmer tone. "I agreed to look at the house only because today is our wedding anniversary, and I want to do something to please my wife. But I told her, and I'm telling you, that I have no intention whatsoever of buying that house."

The moment of silence while everyone pondered his words was broken when Woody said, "Well, when you need my brother-in-law's phone number, let me know."

The buzz in his head increased as everyone returned to their coffee.

The bells jangled and Jerry Selbo entered. Al joined the chorus of hellos to greet the Goose Creek mayor. He answered the greetings with a smile and shrugged out of his jacket as he crossed the room to take an empty chair at Al's table.

"Bit of a nip still in that breeze," he commented, and a collective murmur of agreement answered him.

Lucy set a tall glass of orange juice in front of him. He lifted the glass to his mouth.

"So what's the news on the water tower?" asked Jacob.

The glass halted an inch from Jerry's lips.

42

His eyes widened and flickered sideways toward the counter. Jacob's mouth snapped shut as a heavy silence descended.

Perched on the third stool, Norman Pilkington jerked to attention. "What's 'at? What's goin' on with the tower?"

Jacob winced and mouthed *Sorry* at the mayor, and then hid behind his coffee mug.

Though Al was absent from Goose Creek throughout the week, he stayed well informed on issues related to the town's management because Jerry was a member of the men's group he attended at church on Wednesday nights. This topic had been discussed last week.

The Goose Creek water tower was located one block off of the east end of Main Street. It stood sentinel over the town, a skyscraping monument that symbolized the town's autonomy from the rest of the sprawling county. Three years ago the town hired Norman Pilkington's son to repaint the tower. The only positive comment Al had ever heard from anyone besides Norman was that at least the job was completed on time. The color Little Norm chose was a sickening shade of chartreuse which some compared to baby vomit. The black lettering marched unevenly around the tower's barrel with the *k* in *Creek* taking a disturbing downward slant as though it intended to dive off the platform and escape. Every time Al looked at it, an obsessive itch erupted in the base of his skull and he battled an irrational desire to climb the tower with a can of spray paint and put that *k* out of its misery. Though it had only been three years the paint had begun to flake. Some said Little Norm had bought it at a bargain — which explained the hideous color — while billing the town for premium stuff.

Al had learned to walk through town with his gaze lowered.

Mayor Selbo set his juice down untasted. Only those seated with him saw the slight tremble of his hand. Al felt a flash of sympathy at the mayor's resigned expression. By nature he was a mild-mannered man with a deep desire to please his constituents, and went to great lengths to avoid confrontation. There seemed to be no way to avoid this one, though.

Drawing a deep breath, Jerry turned sideways in his chair to face Norman. "I've received a complaint about the peeling paint on the water tower. It needs to be repainted."

"Last few winters've been hard 'uns on paint. My barn's peelin' too." Norman glanced around and received a few hesitant nods.

Al kept his gaze averted. No doubt everyone in the room shared the same thought. Norman's son had painted his father's tobacco barn around the same time as the water tower.

Norman reached into his jacket pocket and pulled out a cell. "I'll jist give Little Norm a call. See when he can squeeze the job in. He's stayin' right busy these days, ya know."

Norman began to punch numbers on his phone while everyone else shot cautious glances at the mayor.

Jerry's eyes fluttered shut while he sucked in another breath and cleared his throat. "Of course he's welcome to submit a bid, same as everyone else."

A scowl descended over Norman's face, and his finger paused mid-punch. "Whaddya mean, a bid?"

"The town council's announcing a request for bids for the job of painting the water tower. At the April meeting we'll consider the ones we've received and make a decision on who gets awarded the contract."

Norman's spine stiffened. "Are you settin' there tellin' me that you're thinkin' a hirin' somebody 'sides Little Norm?"

"Yes, we are." Al gained new respect for their mayor when the man met Norman's gaze without flinching. "When it comes to spending the town's money we need to avoid the appearance of favoritism. So we're taking bids, and the council will vote on them."

The silence with which Norman received the news set Al shifting in his chair.

"Well." Norman pocketed his phone and slid off his stool. "We'll see 'bout that."

The bells gave an extra-loud jangle when he slammed the door behind him. A collective sigh was expelled from those who remained.

"Sorry, Jerry," Jacob muttered.

With a final glance after Norman, the mayor picked up his orange juice. "Had to happen sooner or later. At least now it's over and done."

Al refrained from answering. Judging by the look on Norman Pilkington's face, the matter was far from over.

CHAPTER FOUR

Al gritted his teeth as his tires bounced through a pothole in the long driveway leading to the Updyke place. The blacktop had so many cracks it looked like a jigsaw puzzle. Jagged lines of weeds pushed through the gaps, some over a foot tall. This disaster of a driveway was a total loss. No amount of patching could repair the mess.

"Oh, Albert, look at that lovely old tree!" Millie turned from the passenger window to fix sparkling eyes on him.

He glanced at the object of her admiration, a giant oak near the corner of the house. The thing had to be at least fifty feet tall. From the looks of it, it hadn't been trimmed since it was planted. Twisted branches poked out from the trunk in all directions, and gnarled roots as big around as his leg crept across the ground toward the porch.

"It's too close to the house," he commented. "See where the branches are rubbing the roof?"

"Those can be trimmed. Just imagine what it will look like in a few weeks when the leaves come in. It'll shade that whole side of the house." She grinned. "That will keep the electricity bill down."

Al ignored her, warming instead to his dire prediction. "Look how it's leaning. It's so old it's probably rotted out inside. At the first strong wind it'll come crashing through the roof."

She gave him the steady look that always preceded a sharp retort, and he braced himself. Her lips tightened but remained still, and she turned back to her window.

So, that's how this would go. She had determined to blithely ignore any rational observations he made. Did she think that attitude would temper his comments? He'd warned her of his intentions last night, and his resolve had not changed.

A car turned into the driveway behind them as Al rolled to a halt near the boarded-up bay window.

"There's Louise, right on time."

Millie unbuckled her seatbelt and opened the car door the moment he cut the engine. Before he'd even gotten out of the car, she trotted over to stand in the unmowed grass, waiting for the realtor to park.

Louise Gaitskill emerged from her shiny red Camry with a folder in one hand and a Starbucks cup in the other. A slender blonde, she would have towered a full head above Millie even without the spike-heeled shoes that contorted her feet into an impossible angle. As the two women hugged, Al shook his head. How her dogs must ache at night when she kicked those ridiculous contrivances off and descended to earth. Thank goodness his wife had better sense.

Of course, the fact that he was here, ready to look through this atrocity of a house, proved that Millie's good sense did not extend to real estate.

Al slid out of his seat and pocketed the keys. Might as well get the ordeal over with.

Millie turned at his approach. "Albert, you know Louise, don't you?"

The realtor shoved a pair of sunglasses up on her head and pasted a bright smile on lips the same color as her Camry. "Of course. Nice to see you again, Mr. Richardson." She tucked the folder beneath one arm and extended her hand.

Al always approached a handshake with a woman with an awkward feeling of caution. How hard should he squeeze? Too much pressure and they might interpret the gesture as a show of male dominance. On the other hand, some ladies approached a handshake like a football tackle, and he never could decide what they were trying to prove with such a firm grip. Others melted limply in the moment of contact, and what did that mean?

"Call me Al," he mumbled as he made a grab at her fingers and gave them a quick shake. Then he shoved his hand into the safety of his trouser pocket.

"Al, then." Another blinding smile. She had obviously bleached her teeth recently. "I'm excited to show you this property. I think you'll agree it has tremendous potential."

He narrowed his eyes. "Potential for what?"

She splayed her free hand wide. "Why, for whatever you want to do with it."

Best get this out in the open right up front. "I don't want to do anything with it. The yard is a shambles, and far too big for us. The roof needs replacing, and it's obvious to anyone with a set of eyes in his head that the house is in a sad state of disrepair. In my opinion it's an antique atrocity."

After a nearly imperceptible pause, Louise's already-bright smile gained a kilowatt or two. "Valid concerns, and definitely something you and Millie need to discuss before making a decision. This property is what we'd call a fixer-upper. Now, if you'll follow me."

She swiveled on one spiked heel and headed for the front steps. Millie trailed after her, leaving Al alone on the crumbling blacktop. So that's how it was going to be. He studied the women chatting amicably while Louise unlocked the front door. Obviously, she and Millie were in cahoots. They'd both decided to ignore his protests and act as though buying this property were an actual possibility. By doing so, no doubt they hoped to dull his determination, to lure him gradually to their way of thinking.

Well, he would not tamely concede the victory in this battle.

Setting his jaw, he marched up the stairs after them.

Louise pushed the door open and stood aside. Millie crossed the threshold and stopped, her gaze sweeping the entry hall. The magnificent staircase dominated the room, demanding the admiration of everyone who entered. It swept upward, turned, and then continued toward the second floor bedrooms. A railing ran alongside a generous landing above. She closed her eyes, picturing the charming Queen Anne sofa she would place at the top of those stairs. A spindly-legged side table with a giant vase of flowers would add the perfect touch. Was there room for a small bookshelf? She'd like to have an assortment of antique books on the shelves, and maybe a second table with a reading lamp. The lampshade would be stained glass, of course.

"Good golly, look at that banister!" Behind her, Albert gave a long, low whistle.

Millie swiveled toward him to voice an enthusiastic comment about the ornate carving on the railings, but bit the words back when she caught sight of his scowl. She turned again to the staircase. "What's wrong with it? I think it's lovely."

"Lovely?" In two strides he crossed the floor — original poplar hardwood that would be gorgeous when refinished — and put a hand on the railing. He gave it a jerk, and turned a look of triumph on her when the wood creaked and wobbled. "It's unsafe. The whole thing needs to be replaced."

"Oh, I doubt that." Behind them, Louise shut the door. "It needs a bit of tightening up for sure, but that's all. Besides, look at the handiwork on those newel posts. You can't buy handcrafted work like that these days. And why would you want to? With a little bit of elbow grease it will be as gorgeous as the day it was built."

Al opened his mouth, and judging by the crevices on his forehead he wasn't about to agree with her. Louise didn't give him a chance, but pulled a sheet of paper out of her folder and thrust it into his hands.

"Here's the spec sheet on the property. I think you'll find all the pertinent information there." She extracted a second sheet and handed it to Millie with a quick smile.

Millie dutifully scanned the page, though she already had a copy tucked away in her magazine rack at home.

A choking sound from Al's direction drew her attention. *"Eight hundred thousand dollars?"*

With his eye sockets open that wide, he resembled Mrs. Tolliver's pug, Chumley.

"Seven ninety-eight," Louise corrected calmly. "After all, it is located in the historic district. And I'm confident the sellers are willing to flex a little on the price point."

"They'd better be willing to flex a lot! This is no fixer-upper. I'd call it a knock-down-and-do-over." Albert turned his bug-eyed stare on Millie. "Six bedrooms? You can't be serious. What in the world would we do with six bedrooms?"

Now was when she needed to remain

levelheaded and stick to her plan. Albert was one of the most intelligent men she knew, and quick to spot what he would no doubt refer to as one of her schemes. One wrong answer at this stage would set his mind down a path she wasn't yet ready to reveal.

She settled herself and replied calmly. "The grandchildren are growing, Albert. We can't have them camping out on the living room floor forever. And of course each married couple deserves a private bedroom when they come for Christmas Eve. Alison's husband won't be stationed in Europe forever, and then we'll be even more crowded."

"So let them go home after dinner! The boys only live a couple of hours away. It's about time for them to develop their own Christmas traditions anyway."

The tears that sprang to her eyes were not forced. The very idea of Christmas morning without her grandbabies padding around the house in their new pajamas was enough to set her lower lip trembling. Not to have them run into Grammy and Papaw's room and leap up onto the bed, screeching excitement and urging Papaw to put on his slippers so they could go to the family room and see what Santa brought? Unthinkable.

Albert seemed unmoved by the appearance of tears in his wife's eyes. If anything, his spine stiffened even more than its already ramrod-stubborn posture. "A six thousand square foot house is absolutely ridiculous for a retired couple. Even the twenty-two hundred we have now is more than an aging couple like us needs. But at least ours is all on one level."

Aging couple?

Louise saved her from what may have been a sharp reply by stepping smoothly between them. "Let's take a look at the front sitting room, shall we?" The noise of her heels striking the scarred hardwood sounded magnified in the awkward silence. "Just look at the scrollwork on the lintel over the doorway. Isn't that stunning?"

She pushed open a heavy wooden door. When Millie and Violet toured the house a few days ago, they'd agreed this door should be painted white, along with the tall baseboards and other trim. Before Millie entered the sitting room she saw Albert reach over and slip a finger beneath a piece of peeling wallpaper. His lips twisted and he shook his head.

"Wallpaper is easily replaced," she informed him as she swept past.

Inside the doorway she stepped aside and

let the room work its magic on her again. This room would be the heart of their home. The tall ceilings created a spacious feeling, and the ornate crown molding flooded the room with elegance. When this busy old wallpaper was stripped off and the walls painted a charming robin's-egg blue, the carved mantle on the fireplace would become a lovely centerpiece to draw the eye. The chandelier was exquisite; those crystals would sparkle like diamonds when they were cleaned. And the bay window! She crossed the room and sank onto a dingy and faded window seat.

A puff of dust rose and set her to coughing. With a look of alarm, Albert covered his mouth with his shirt collar. "I wouldn't breathe in here if I were you. With that broken window, I'll bet the place is full of mold. Might even be black mold. It'll get in your lungs."

"A mold test is always advisable before you buy one of these historic homes." Standing beside the fireplace, Louise sipped from her coffee cup. "But I haven't seen any sign of mold. That window has been tightly secured."

Unconvinced, Albert cast one more glance around the room and made a hasty exit, his mouth still covered. Millie let out a sigh.

He seemed determined to display his stubborn streak today. Though she'd fully expected resistance, in the recesses of her mind she'd harbored a hope that he would fall in love with the house when he saw it. Obviously, that wasn't going to happen.

Oh, well. That just made the task a little more difficult. She heaved herself off the window seat and headed after her husband.

As the tour dragged on, Al fell silent. He could find no new words to describe his opinions after he'd overused *dismal, disaster,* and *catastrophe-in-the-making* to the point that even Louise's ever-present smile had begun to twitch with annoyance whenever he voiced an opinion. The hopelessness of this architectural calamity transformed his initial pessimism into a gloomy melancholy. How in the world could Millie wade through all the dust and gaze down at the crumbling stone fireplaces — *seven* of them, for cryin' out loud! — and not want to run shrieking to the car?

"And here's one of my favorite features of this property," Louise announced as she twisted the lock on a set of heavily-draped French doors in the rear wall of the dining room. "Just look at this verandah."

Millie gasped aloud, folding her hands

beneath her chin in obvious delight. Glumly, Al followed her outside. He stepped onto a cracked flagstone that shifted beneath his shoe, and he wavered to regain his balance.

"Careful there, Al," Louise cautioned. "Some of these pavers aren't in the best shape. But I'm sure you'll agree that with some TLC and a little elbow grease, the potential for this outdoor space is practically limitless."

He bit back a sharp retort about there not being enough elbows in the entire town to take on this project.

Actually, this was a nice back porch. It was deep and covered and ran the whole length of the house, with columns spaced evenly to support the roof. The waist-high railing needed to be replaced, of course — was there anything in this house that didn't? — but it added the homey touch he'd been unable to achieve on his own redwood deck. Maybe he should have reconsidered the inexpensive metal awning he'd had installed over his deck. This sturdy roof made the patio feel like an extension of the house. Like the front yard, the lawn back here was in desperate need of tending. But the mature oaks scattered across the property promised an abundance of shady retreats during hot summer days. He could almost see himself parked beneath that big one in the center, a glass of lemonade in one hand, a book open on his lap and bullfrogs croaking from the pond behind him.

Millie glided toward the railing, her gaze rapturous. "Just look at the lake! It's beautiful."

"Pond," Al corrected automatically.

"Whatever. It's big enough for a paddle boat." She turned toward him, eyes shining. "I can see us floating out there, me wearing a sundress and a big floppy hat while you read poetry to me like you did when we were dating."

He could have come up with a suitable rejoinder, only at the moment his mind had conjured a memory of the time she referred to. She had looked so adorable in that yellow dress and hat, and she'd gazed at him with love in her eyes. That was the day he'd decided to marry her.

He cleared his throat. "If you want poetry, I'll read it from the comfort of my recliner. That way we won't get skin cancer from overexposure to the sun."

Judging by the sudden snap of her teeth and narrowing of her eyes, that comment had tipped the scales. She didn't bother to mask her annoyance as her chin jutted forward and she turned pointedly away from him.

The realtor avoided eye contact with either of them. "Let's have a look at the basement, shall we?"

What was the point? Anniversary or not, Al was done. They'd already wasted an hour of their Saturday tromping all over the place. Millie was mad at him, as he'd known she would be, so the rest of the day would be awkward and uncomfortable.

"Go ahead," Al told them. "I'll wait in the car."

Millie turned a surprised look his way. "You don't want to see the basement?"

He replied as patiently as he could. "I didn't want to see any of it. I agreed only to make you happy." A longsuffering tone crept into his voice. "Apparently that attempt was a failure, so I see no reason to keep trying."

She stared at him for a long moment, her expression unreadable. A battle was taking place inside that head of hers, probably weighing the idea of blasting him with a sharp reply against the awkwardness of succumbing to an argument in front of an outsider. Propriety won, because all she did was nod once before she disappeared into the house. Louise awarded him one of her perky smiles and followed her inside.

When the door clicked shut, an empty silence pressed on his ears. How could he salvage what was left of the day and smooth her ruffled feathers? A gift? Flowers? No, she might construe those as an apology, and he refused to apologize for acting as the voice of reason. In fact, if anyone had a right to be angry, it was him. She should be trying to come up with a way to pacify him, not the other way around.

Movement near the big tree in the center of the yard caught his eye. A squirrel scampered across the ground. No, not one. Three squirrels. Just as he'd suspected, the place was infested with the pesky things.

His resolve thus strengthened, he strode around the side of the house to wait in the car.

CHAPTER FIVE

"Honestly, Violet, I've never seen him more stubborn." Millie leaned closer, dodging a hairspray-cemented curl to speak quietly in her friend's ear. "It was so embarrassing for Louise to see him acting like a cantankerous old poop."

They stood close together on the sidewalk outside the Woodview Community Church, waiting for the rest of their group. A line formed inside the church, worshippers waiting to shake Reverend Hollister's hand before they trickled out into the sunshine. On fine spring days most of the congregation walked to church. Today was the first time this year the weather had cooperated.

"He can be stubborn as a mule." Violet nodded sagely.

Millie spared a smile for Cheryl Lawson, who was attempting to wrangle her boys down the walkway. "It wasn't just stubbornness," she told Violet. "It was his whole demeanor. He never smiled once. Even when he wasn't pointing out an endless list of repairs that would need to be done, he scowled the whole time. I knew he would be pessimistic, but I expected he would at least be polite."

"What did he think of the kitchen?" Violet asked. "Surely he admired that big stone fireplace."

"He pointed out the crumbling mortar and said he had no idea where to find a competent stone mason who could fix it for less than five hundred dollars." Millie twisted her lips. "I think he was keeping a running total of all the repairs in his mind during the whole tour."

Violet shook her head. "Sounds like my Frank, God rest his soul. He was tighter than bark on a log."

Millie spied Albert shaking the Reverend's hand. He descended the steps and joined a small cluster of people talking with Doc and Lizzie Forsythe on the sidewalk. "There he is. Don't mention the house, okay?"

"My lips are sealed." Violet used her fingers to twist an imaginary lock on her thin lips. "I won't let the cat out of the bag. I'll be quiet as a church mouse." She smiled, obviously pleased at the opportunity to use three appropriate clichés at once.

They joined the group in time to hear Jacob Pulliam say, "I can't believe you're really gonna do it."

"You act like this is a surprise." Doc nodded a greeting at Millie and Violet as he answered. "I've been talking about retiring for years."

"He's been *promising* for years," Lizzie corrected with a smile at her husband. "Ever since his mother moved to Florida. It's long overdue, if you ask me."

Millie looked at her boss. "Does that mean the meeting the other night went well?" She'd known a potential buyer was coming to see the animal clinic, but since she didn't work on Saturdays she hadn't heard how things turned out.

Doc nodded. "She called last night with an offer."

"She?" Fred Rightmier's eyebrows arched high on his shiny red forehead. "You're selling out to a *woman*?"

Violet jerked upright. "You don't think a woman can be a veterinarian?"

Fred didn't back down under her sharp stare. " 'Course they can, but we're used to a guy, is all. Not sure Goose Creek's ready for a woman doctor, even an animal doctor."

"Careful, Fred," cautioned Albert mildly.

"Your narrowmindedness is showing."

Doc clapped a hand on Fred's arm. "Give her a chance, will you? She's going to be a good vet." He held a hand out to Lizzie. "Ready?"

Watching the couple stroll hand-in-hand down the sidewalk, Millie's irritation with Albert softened. Yes, he was irksome at times, but she loved him. In twenty years, she fully intended to be walking down this street, holding his hand, just like Doc and Lizzie.

The group headed out and bid Fred goodbye when he turned left on Cross Street. At the next intersection, Jacob and Doris veered off, leaving Millie, Albert, and Violet to cover the last block on their own.

"Would you like to come for lunch?" Millie asked her neighbor when they reached Mulberry Avenue. "We're having leftover roast beef from last night."

Before Violet could answer, Albert spoke. "Actually, we're not having lunch at home today. We're going out."

Surprised, she looked at him. "We are? Where?"

"It's a secret."

She studied him. A smile hovered around his lips, giving him a satisfied air. In fact, he looked quite pleased with himself. She felt a rush of warmth toward him. No doubt this lunch was an attempt to apologize for his brusqueness yesterday. He knew she was still irritated with him, and this was his way of making amends. How sweet.

"I'll take a rain check then," Violet said as she veered off the sidewalk toward her front door. "Call me later."

Naturally, she would expect a full report on Albert's secret plans.

Millie waved. "I will."

Al sat on the edge of the dock and swung his feet into the canoe. He planted his weight and tested his balance before reaching up to take the picnic basket from Millie.

"I still can't believe it." Happy tears sparkled in her eyes as she handed the basket down to him. "When did you arrange this?"

"Last night, while you were out front talking to Violet. It was too late to go then, on our actual anniversary. I'm sorry I didn't think of it earlier in the day."

He truly was sorry. Had he remembered about this manmade lake on the outskirts of Lexington earlier, he might have spared himself the misery of his wife's tight-lipped silence over the most uncomfortable anniversary dinner they'd ever spent. He drove by this neighborhood twice a day on his commute, and knew his coworker had built one of the giant new homes that circled the lake. Last summer Ben had showed him pictures of his kids paddling their inflatable canoe around the lake. All it had taken was a phone call, and he received permission to borrow the canoe for a few hours. Ben had blown it up with his air compressor last night, and his wife had even volunteered to pack a picnic lunch for them so he wouldn't have to tell Millie of the plans until they arrived.

Judging by her tearful and almost speechless reaction, this surprise would go a long way toward restoring matrimonial harmony in the Richardson home.

"Don't apologize," she told him. "This just makes our anniversary last longer."

The basket stowed behind his bench seat, he helped her down from the dock. The canoe pitched unsteadily, and she emitted a nervous giggle. "It's not as sturdy as a rowboat."

"No indeed."

Al held on to the dock to steady the craft while she got settled on her bench. She sat facing him, the way she would in a regular boat. The seats were so close together they had to sit almost sideways, knees pointing at opposite angles. If Ben's family were watching from their house, no doubt they were enjoying a good laugh at the thought that the old folks didn't know what they were doing. They'd be wrong. This wasn't a canoe lesson. It was a date.

When they felt comfortable with their balance, Al took up the plastic paddle and shoved off. The craft drifted slowly away from shore. He plunged the blade into the water and pulled. The canoe shot across the smooth surface, and then Millie's end swerved inward. Another stroke, this one not quite as swift, and their circle continued, pointing them toward the shore.

"It might take me a minute to get the hang of this." Al lifted the paddle and swung it to the other side.

"Oh!" A surprised exclamation escaped her lips, and she ducked forward. The paddle blade swept over her head, narrowly missing her skull, and the canoe teetered unsteadily.

"Sorry," Al muttered.

He plunged the oar into the water, feeling the drag on his shoulders as the canoe's spin halted. A few experimental strokes later, he achieved the right amount of effort, and the boat moved more or less smoothly toward the center of the lake.

"There." Satisfied, he slid the paddle beneath their seats. Though he'd been glad of his jacket a moment before, the exertion warmed him enough to produce a sheen of sweat on the back of his neck. No doubt his muscles would complain about the unaccustomed activity later.

"Nicely done," Millie told him.

"Thank you." He glanced around. Houses surrounded the lake, all of them big and expensive-looking with windows facing their direction. "Not as private as the last time, I'm afraid."

"But every bit as romantic." The smile she gave him was even more dazzling than the sunlight that sparkled on the gently rippling water.

When they had eaten the sandwiches and carrots dipped in ranch dressing provided by Ben's wife, Al pulled a small book of poetry from his pocket.

She glanced at the cover, and her expression became soft. "Robert Burns. You remember."

"Of course I remember." He turned to the page he'd marked this morning. "A Red Red Rose." The poem that had defined their love so beautifully forty years before was even more perfect now. When he reached the third verse, his voice became husky.

69

Till a' the seas gang dry, my dear,
And the rocks melt wi' the sun;
I will luve thee still, my dear
While the sands o' life shall run.

She leaned forward and pressed her finger-
tips to his cheek, her gaze soft. "Thank you
for bringing me here. I'm sorry I was so
cranky last night."

"I'm sorry too." He looked down at the
book to turn a page. When he raised his gaze
again, her smile had taken on a slightly rigid
look. "What?"

"Do you mean you're sorry you were
cranky last night, or you're sorry I was
cranky?"

He cocked his head, considering. "Both, I
guess."

Wrong answer. Her nostrils flared the way
they did when she was angry, and the air
between them dropped a frosty fifteen degrees.

A bit of backpedaling was definitely in
order.

"What I mean is, we were both upset and
I'm sorry that ruined our anniversary dinner." No change in her expression. "Not
that the dinner was ruined. The food was
wonderful, as always. It's the mood that was
ruined, and that wasn't your fault." He

rushed on, lest she think he was conceding his position. "Or mine either. It was because of that blasted house."

"The *blasted house* that I happen to love," she shot back.

Her tone grated on his nerves. "That house is a disaster. It's falling apart. You saw it with your own eyes. I was afraid to walk through the place without a hardhat."

"Don't be ridiculous," she snapped. "Peeling wallpaper doesn't constitute a disaster, and it certainly isn't dangerous."

"Rotted roof trusses are."

"How do you know the trusses are rotten? You didn't even go into the attic." Her lips pressed into a hard line.

With an effort, Al managed to reply in an even, if tight, tone. "The price is eight hundred thousand dollars, Millie. We can't afford it."

"They would take five fifty."

Surprised, Al's irritation receded a fraction. That was more than thirty percent below the asking price. "Why would the Updykes let their family home go for so little?"

"I told you the other day. They need money."

He narrowed his eyes. "Did Louise tell you what they'd settle for?" If so, the woman should have her real estate license revoked for unethical practices.

But Millie shook her head. "Louise told me the Updyke brothers would entertain any offer, but Violet heard the number from Cheryl, who got it from Laura, who is still friends with Sammy Updyke's wife."

A fairly reliable chain of information, he had to admit. The number had probably been reduced a few times to inflate the juiciness of the gossip, but even if the Updykes' actual bottom price was six hundred thousand, that would be twenty-five percent lower than —

He jerked upright, causing the canoe to wobble. What was he *thinking*?

"The repairs would probably be at least a hundred thousand," he told his wife.

"We could do a lot of the work ourselves." She leaned toward him and planted her elbows on her knees. "My friends and I can strip the wallpaper, and we can certainly do the painting. You're handy with a hammer and screwdriver, so you can do a lot of the fixing up yourself. For the bigger stuff, Laura knows a young man over in Frankfort who just started his own home repair business. She says he's very good and his rates are reasonable."

Good golly, she had the whole thing planned already. This was no spur-of-the-moment idea. She'd spent time looking into it.

"But Millie, we don't *need* six bedrooms and seven fireplaces. And while I admit that back porch would be nice —"

"I knew you'd love that," she put in, her tone bright with excitement.

Al continued. "The fact is we can't afford to wipe out our savings three years before we retire."

"It wouldn't wipe out our savings."

True. They had always lived frugally, and had been planning for retirement from the early years of their marriage. "It would certainly put a huge dent in them."

She averted her gaze toward the gently rippling water beside them. "What if the house *made* money for us?"

"Huh?"

"Once we got it fixed up, I think the Up-dyke house would pay for itself."

"You mean, fix it up and resell it? Like that TV show, *Flip or Flop*?"

"No." One delicate finger trailed across the canoe's rubber edge as she spoke. "I mean we could open a bed and breakfast."

In the silence that followed, Al replayed the words in his mind. Individually, he understood every one, but strung together like that, they made no sense. Surely his wife, the love of his life, his levelheaded Millie, had not just suggested that they launch a new business at the time when they were finally ready to kick back and enjoy themselves.

"Excuse me." He put a finger in his ear and shook it dramatically. "For a moment I thought you said you wanted to open a hotel."

"Not a hotel. A bed and breakfast." She leaned toward him, enthusiasm dancing in her eyes. "I've always wanted to run one. You know how I love to entertain, and I have such marvelous decorating ideas. It would be tremendous fun, like having houseguests every night."

Definitely not his idea of fun. "Who in their right mind would want to visit Goose Creek?"

"Horse race enthusiasts," she replied. "Keeneland Race Course is just fifteen miles away, and the Kentucky Horse Park, and all the thoroughbred farms, and of course there's the Derby. And all the wineries in the area, and the Bourbon Trail. And the state capital in Frankfort. Besides, people would love the chance to stay in a Victorian house on a beautiful property."

Who *was* this woman?

He reached out and gripped her shoulders.

"Millie, listen to yourself. We're about to *retire.* Our house is paid for, our kids grown. We have no commitments, nothing to tie us down. I want to travel, to visit places we've never seen. The Grand Canyon. Florida. San Francisco. Yellowstone and Old Faithful." He released her and waved his hands expansively. "There's a whole country full of places we've never been to, just waiting for us to discover them."

"Albert, be reasonable. Do you know how much airline tickets are these days? And hotel rooms?"

"I do. That's why we'd buy a motor home."

She blinked. "A what?"

"A motor home. An RV." He poured his enthusiasm into a wide smile. "I've been looking into them, and I think we can pick up a really nice used one when we're ready to buy."

Millie sat up straight. "I refuse to spend my retirement traipsing around the country in a trailer. I gave up camping years ago."

"It's not like tent camping," he explained. "It's more like —"

"I won't do it." She folded her arms across her chest with a slap. "End of discussion."

Al's irritation returned with a vengeance. "Oh, I forgot. You'd rather bankrupt us buying an ancient money pit and turn us into servants for pampered rich people who enjoy throwing their money away on horse races."

"At least we'd sleep in a proper bed every night," she snapped.

A noise penetrated the angry blood pounding in Al's ears. Voices. Someone was shouting at them. He pulled his glare away from Millie to look over his shoulder. On the shore stood Ben and his wife, along with two preteen boys. They were all waving their hands in the air, yelling his name.

"What's wrong with them?" Millie asked in a tone only slightly less aggravated.

"I don't know." He cupped his hands around his mouth and shouted. "What's the problem?"

"We forgot to tell you about the —"

His warning was drowned out by a loud noise. Al whipped around to locate the source. The canoe floated near the center of the lake, a few feet from an odd-looking pipe that protruded a foot or so from the surface.

A fountain.

Water gushed from the pipe and leaped twelve feet into the air before succumbing to gravity. The resulting shower was quite beautiful glistening in the sunlight above their heads.

It was also very cold.

CHAPTER SIX

Susan paused for a moment on the doorstep of the Goose Creek Animal Clinic to brush at a crease in her lab coat. What was behind this unaccustomed twinge of nerves? Her education was finished, her training thorough, and her reference materials extensive. As Daddy assured her on the phone last night, there was nothing she would encounter in any Goose Creek pet that she couldn't handle. Thus fortified, she drew in a breath and reached for the knob.

The door jerked inward. She caught a glimpse of black fur an instant before a weight slammed into her chest. Thrown backward, her foot grappled for balance but instead of the porch found only air. For a moment she was airborn and then, with a thud that knocked the breath from her lungs, she landed on her backside in the grass and lay still, gasping.

"Boomer, no! Bad dog! *Baaad* dog."

A commanding female voice penetrated the fog in her oxygen-deprived brain. At the same moment, she realized why she couldn't breathe. There was a bear on her chest.

The creature was heaved backward and, blinking to clear her vision, she struggled to sit up. Not a bear. A dog. A *giant* dog, straining at the end of a leash, a thick string of slime dangling from one glistening jowl.

The other end of the leash was held by a woman with a stump-shaped body and a cap of steel-gray hair. She peered over the top of the dog's head at Susan, and then turned to yell over her shoulder in a voice that rivaled a lumberjack's.

"Millie, you'd best get on out here. Boomer's done kilt the new doc."

Another woman bustled through the doorway, caught sight of Susan, and rushed forward. "Oh my goodness. Are you hurt? Should we call 911?"

Susan lay there a moment, assessing her injuries. Arms and legs all worked. Her backside had taken the brunt of her weight and she'd probably have a bruise, but nothing felt broken. Cautiously, she struggled to sit up. Thank goodness she'd landed on grass instead of the sidewalk.

"Maybe you should stay there for a minute," the newcomer advised, her concerned gaze sweeping over Susan. "I'll go get Doc."

"No, I'm fine. I was just . . . surprised."

How embarrassing. She hadn't even stepped foot through the door of her new clinic and already she'd caused a scene. Moving slowly, she stood and cast a cautious eye toward her attacker, who had stopped straining at the leash and now sat calmly watching her.

"It's a Newfoundland." She'd never seen one in person but knew about the big dogs, of course. Prone to medial carthal pocket syndrome due to the shape of the gigantic head, though this one showed no sign of the eye condition. Also prone to hip dysplasia, like all large breeds. Judging by this creature's agility, that wasn't a problem either.

"Yep," the owner replied in her gravelly voice. "Always wanted a Newfie. No sissypants froufrou pup for me. Gimme a real dog." The woman cocked her head sideways and looked Susan up and down. "So you're the new doc. Not too sturdy on your feet, are you?"

Susan resisted the urge to bristle, and instead pasted on a professionally pleasant expression. "Yes, I'm Dr. Jeffries." She tentatively extended her fingers for the dog to sniff. "And I've already met Boomer.

We're going to get along fine, aren't we, boy?"

Boomer's owner twisted her thin lips. "We'll think on it." She looped the leash once more around her hand before heading down the sidewalk. "C'mon, Boomer."

The pair marched toward the parking lot while the other lady stepped to her side.

"Don't worry about Edith. She'll come around." She gave a pleasant smile. "I'm Millie Richardson, your morning receptionist. Come on inside and I'll get the lint roller."

Susan glanced down to find her white lab coat covered in black hair and fell into step behind the receptionist. Inside, Millie circled around the desk and rummaged in a drawer. She peeled off the outer paper of a lint roller to reveal a clean sticky layer and handed it to Susan, who began the cleanup process.

She glanced around while she rolled. The waiting rooms were empty. Not a good sign.

"Is it a slow morning?" she asked.

"Not really. Doc's in exam room one checking on a kitty with a vomiting problem, and Larry Greely's waiting in room two with Bella."

Susan rolled the last piece of hair and returned the roller to Millie. "Bella?"

"His bird dog. Her first litter's due in a few weeks, and he's an anxious grandpa." The woman's grin was infectious, and Susan found herself smiling back.

"Maybe I should go introduce myself."

She started toward the back, but Millie stepped in front of her on the pretext of swiping the roller at her left sleeve.

"It might be a good idea to let Doc introduce you." She stepped back to examine her work, and then gave an apologetic shrug. "Doc and Larry are old friends."

Susan saw the logic in that and nodded. She was about to head for exam room one to be introduced to the owner of the feline with the intestinal problem when the door leading to the back opened. An elderly woman carrying a white longhaired cat emerged, followed by Dr. Forsythe.

"You try that trick with the can in his bowl. That'll force him to eat slower."

"I will, Doc. Thank you." She caught sight of Susan and interest flooded her features. "Is this the new veterinarian?"

"Indeed it is." Dr. Forsythe came forward with a welcoming smile to shake her hand. "Delores Barnes, allow me to introduce Dr. Susan Jeffries." He stroked the back of the cat. "And this fine fellow is Arnold."

"He's named after my late husband, who

detested cats." Mrs. Barnes' eyes twinkled. "I wasn't allowed to have one until he passed. Now I have four."

Susan couldn't come up with a safe answer, so instead she busied herself in stroking the cat's soft fur. "He's a beautiful feline."

"Here." The elderly lady thrust the animal into Susan's arms. "You can hold him while I write the check."

Though the fluffy double coat of fur made the cat look huge, Arnold felt light in Susan's arms. He seemed completely unconcerned at being held by a stranger. She ran her fingers down his spine, noting the position of the vertebrae. Nothing out of place. He remained limp as she probed the hip joint and traced the bones in his leg down to his rear paw. Then she repeated the examination on his front leg, splaying his toes.

"Oh! Goodness." She raised her gaze to Dr. Forsythe, who was grinning. "I've never seen one."

Mrs. Barnes tore a check from her checkbook and handed it across the reception counter to Millie before turning an inquisitive gaze her way. "You've never seen a cat, dear?"

Susan chuckled. "No, ma'am, I mean I've

never seen a polydactyl cat."

The elderly woman looked blank.

"She means a cat with six toes," Dr. Forsythe explained.

Mrs. Barnes' expression cleared. "Ah."

"I've studied the condition, of course." Susan splayed Arnold's toes, noting the position of the sixth digit. "It's a congenital physical anomaly."

"A what?"

"A mutation," Susan explained, warming to the subject. "As such, some well-regarded sources strongly discourage breeding so as not to pass on the deformity. Sterilization is encouraged."

She started to spread Arnold's rear legs to see if the procedure had been performed, but the cat was jerked roughly from her arms. Surprised, she looked up into Mrs. Barnes' fiery gaze.

"Arnold is *not* a mutant!" With an indignant huff, the woman whirled and stalked toward the door.

"I didn't mean to imply he was a mutant." Susan hurried after her. "Mrs. Barnes, all I meant was —"

Her explanation went unheard. The door slammed in her face.

She turned to find Millie giving her a pitying look.

Dr. Forsythe shook his head slowly. "We're kind of fond of our six-toed friends around here. You might want to keep that in mind."

Stunned, Susan could only nod.

By mid-morning Susan was almost ready to concede defeat to the extreme obduracy of Goose Creek pet owners. Larry Greely not only refused to let her touch his precious bird dog, he banished her from the room when Dr. Forsythe began his examination, claiming, "Bella, she don't cotton to strangers." From the deeply mistrustful way the man watched her, it appeared Bella wasn't the only one.

Mr. Greely's reservations about newcomers were repeated time and again. Apparently the pet-owning residents of Goose Creek maintained an active communication line, and it must have been buzzing all morning. Just after noon Susan emerged from the back to the reception area in time to hear one lady inform Millie in an outraged tone, ". . . called Arnold a deformed mutant and wanted to cut his toe off!"

Millie corrected the misinformation, but the lady insisted that only Dr. Forsythe be allowed to trim her dachshund's toenails.

After the third pet owner informed Susan, "Trigger doesn't like to be touched by people he doesn't know," she resigned herself to watching from a corner while Doc, as everyone called him, conducted the examinations. The people clearly admired and trusted him.

He certainly did know his patients. As his fingers glided over their furry little bodies he kept up a running monologue, informing Susan of the details surrounding each animal's history from birth all the way to last week. Not once did she see him refer to a chart. She scribbled furiously in her notepad as he spoke. By the time she went to bed tonight she vowed to commit every detail to memory. The next time these animals visited the clinic, she would *not* be a stranger.

That is, if any of them ever returned. She tried to ignore the tug of gloom as, one by one, they bid farewell to Doc and even Millie with words that held a note of finality. One lady even hesitated in the doorway before exiting, her gaze circling the reception area, and said wistfully, "What a shame. I've always liked this place."

When Daddy called tonight, she'd ask his advice. After all, as the primary funder of her new business, he had a right to know the challenges she faced. And maybe he'd be able to offer a helpful suggestion or two.

The dog-shaped clock on the wall above the reception desk had just barked eleven times when the front door opened. Seated in the Kuddly Kittie room, Susan looked up from her perusal of a *Cat Fancy* magazine. Maybe she'd be allowed to examine *this* animal. Doc had announced his intention to run down the street for a soda, leaving her in charge for a few minutes, but the two pet owners who arrived after he left had informed her that they weren't in a hurry. They were currently installed in exam rooms one and two, waiting for Doc's return.

The man who entered wore a scowl that rested naturally on his heavy-browed features. And he had no pet in evidence. Instead, he carried a spiral notebook.

Millie smiled a greeting. "Hello, Norman. I heard you might be stopping by."

"Figgered." The man slumped forward and slammed his notebook down on the counter. "You-uns gonna sign?"

The pleasant expression on the receptionist's face did not change. "I've spoken with Albert, and we'd prefer not to get involved."

Norman emitted a low-throated growl. "Live here, doncha? Gotta get involved. Cain't let the government tell us how we're gonna live. Got forty-three names right here says I ain't the only one who thinks so."

Susan lowered the magazine to her lap. The man was circulating a petition of some sort.

"The Council isn't trying to tell us how to live." The gently chiding tone Millie used might have been appropriate for a kindergarten teacher explaining why he must share the crayons with the other children. "They're only trying to make a fair decision."

"Bah! They's giving business to outsiders. Creeker money ought to stay in the Creek, where it'll do some good for the town."

Her ears perked up. Whatever the issue was, if it concerned Goose Creek, it concerned her business. She stood and dropped the magazine into the wall rack on her way to join the conversation at the counter.

"Hello." She gave the man a bright smile and extended her hand. "I'm Dr. Susan Jeffries."

The man's scowl deepened, his eyebrows descending to almost obscure his close-set eyes. "The new animal doc?"

"That's right. And as a new business owner in Goose Creek, I'm interested in hearing what you have to say."

Millie rolled her desk chair to one side so she was behind Norman. Wide-eyed, she began a silent pantomime, shaking her head and holding a finger over her lips. What did the woman mean? Surely she didn't have a problem with her new boss becoming civic-minded.

Susan's gaze jerked back to Norman when he raised a crooked finger and jabbed it toward her face. "You are jest what I'm talkin' about. Somebody ought to take Doc out behind the barn and wallop him a good un."

The grease-caked fingernail stabbed alarmingly close to Susan's nose, and she took an involuntary step backward. "Excuse me?"

"Ain't no excuse for ye, comin' in here expecting us to hand over our hard-earned money so's you can take it back to wherever you're from, when we got people right here in this town who's trying to make a decent living."

"B-but I'm moving to Goose Creek. As soon as I find a place to live I'm going to break my lease and move here."

"Yeah?" The man dismissed her protest with a wave of the accusing finger. "Don't be too quick about that. They's lots of Creekers don't take kindly to strangers, even strangers with fancy degrees."

With a final glare, the man whirled and

stomped away. The door slammed behind him.

Dumbfounded, Susan stared at the swinging mini blinds. After her reception from the Goose Creek pet owners she'd met today, his words rang like the gongs of prophecy in her ears.

"Don't mind Norman." Millie glanced toward the door. "The town council has wedged a burr under his saddle. It's nothing to do with you. Do you drink tea, dear?"

"What?" Susan shook her head and turned to the receptionist. "Um, yes. Sometimes."

Millie opened a drawer and extracted a box of chamomile. "I'll just zap some water in the microwave and we'll have a cuppa while I explain."

CHAPTER SEVEN

Al stared morosely at the figures displayed on his computer monitor. His retirement accounts, so carefully managed over the years, were in danger of being squandered. If he conceded to this scheme of Millie's, he'd be working for the rest of his life just to put food on their table and keep a roof over their heads. A roof that would probably decimate at least one of his IRA accounts.

A face appeared over the top of the cubicle wall and fixed him with a smirky grin. " 'Sup, Bert?"

Al set his teeth. Several years ago he'd stopped reacting to Franklin Thacker's attempt to needle him by calling him *Bert.* Correcting the guy merely resulted in that irritating guffaw of his. Retaliation had also proved ineffective, since addressing his cubicle neighbor as *Lin* only encouraged him. Instead, Al had settled into an approach of patient endurance. Thacker was a temporary annoyance, and best treated as such.

"Working." He clipped the word short and stared solidly at his monitor. Sometimes ignoring Thacker made him go away.

Unfortunately, not today.

The man folded his arms across the top of the cubicle and rested his chin on them. "Heard you and the little woman took a boat ride yesterday."

Uh oh. Here it came. He'd been waiting all day for the canoe story to make its way around the office. Al turned his expression to stone and did not respond.

"Real romantic, I heard. A picnic on the water and all. Yep. Only one thing, though." Thacker's smirk deepened. "Next time you want to score points with the missus, instead of a ham sandwich you might want to give her an umbrella."

He erupted into guffaws punctuated by snorts. To make matters worse, answering chuckles sounded from within several of the nearby cubicles. Al drowned them out with the noise of his teeth grinding against one another.

Still snorting, Thacker withdrew.

If Al had to pinpoint one single thing he would enjoy most about his long-anticipated retirement, it was that he would never have to lay eyes on Franklin Thacker again.

"I'm worried about her," Millie told Violet that afternoon. "When I left the clinic at noon she looked so down."

Seated at the table in Millie's comfy kitchen, the ladies were engaged in a ritual they practiced on Mondays and Thursdays: afternoon tea with fancy treats just like the queen of England had every day. The mini scone recipe she'd found in an old church cookbook — and tweaked, of course — had turned out better than she hoped.

Violet plucked a second scone from the middle tier of the silver serving tray. "You know how Creekers are about outsiders. That gal is about as welcome here as a skunk at a lawn party."

Unfortunately, Violet was correct. With a sigh, Millie helped herself to another cucumber-and-cream-cheese finger sand-wich. "She's so young. If people don't ac-cept her immediately, I'm afraid she'll take it personally."

"Timid as a field mouse, is she?"

"No, not timid." Millie dismembered her sandwich and wiped off the excess cheese. Violet always slathered on too much for her taste. "She's rather intense. Pays very close attention when people talk, and doesn't smile much."

"Gets along better with animals than with people," Violet observed with more insight than usual.

"Exactly. At least, I imagine so. The poor girl wasn't given much chance to interact with the animals. Delores must have called everyone in town the moment she got home." Millie replaced the top slice of rye and wiped cream cheese from her knife on the side of her hand-painted dessert plate. "I don't know what we'll do when Doc and Lizzie move away. I'm afraid everyone will take their pets to a vet in Lexington."

Violet cocked her head and examined her half-eaten scone. "Maybe I'll bite the bullet and get me a cat. I've been thinking of it for some time."

The idea of a cat sharpening its claws on Violet's already-worn sofa and leaping from one dusty, cluttered table to the next sent a shiver down Millie's back. Though Violet was her best friend in the world, she was not an immaculate housekeeper.

Sometimes friendship required brutal honesty. She set down her sandwich and leaned across the table to catch her friend's eye. "You don't vacuum often enough, dear. Think of the cat hair."

Violet shrugged, not offended in the slightest. "You're probably right. Besides, Rufus wouldn't like living next door to a cat. I'm sure they'd fight" — she grinned — "like cats and dogs."

With a moan, Millie retrieved her sandwich. "If you mention rain at this point," she told her friend, "I will shove the rest of these scones in your mouth."

Violet laughed and reached for her teacup. "We'll have to come up with another way to help your new boss. Perhaps a postcard giving every pet a free checkup?"

Actually, that wasn't a bad idea. "We'd have to put an expiration date on it. We don't want the poor girl conducting free exams for the next five years."

"And a limit," Violet warned. "One pet per household. Otherwise John Wayne will bring all fourteen of his hounds."

The more she considered the idea of an introductory special offer, the more Millie liked it. "You know, that might work. I'll mention it to her and Doc tomorrow." She sipped fragrant tea, Earl Grey this time, and set her dainty cup in its saucer.

Violet gathered a handful of nuts from the top serving tier. "Has Al called today?"

At the mention of her husband's name, Millie's appetite fled. She set her unfinished sandwich down again and slid her plate away. "No, and I expected him to call and apologize for being such a grouch all evening."

"I'm sorry." Her friend gave her an understanding smile and then lowered her gaze. "What's good for the goose is good for the gander, you know. And vicey-versa."

True, she could have called Albert at the office with her own apology. After all, she hadn't been very friendly last night either. Their cold shower in the lake had done nothing to cool her anger, and she'd maintained a rigid posture all the way home, staring out the passenger window with her back turned to her husband as far as the seatbelt would allow. For the first time in decades, they had gone to bed without speaking. Even now, the thought of their disagreement fanned angry embers that had not quite burned themselves out.

"Imagine!" she blurted. "Me, roaming around the country in a travel trailer. Cooking on a camp stove and showering in a closet. Where did he come up with such an idea?"

"Men are from Mars." Violet nodded sagely. "And women —"

"— are from Venus. Yes, I know." She smiled to take the sting out of her tone. If she couldn't get a handle on her temper before Albert got home from work, tonight would be a miserable repeat of last night. With a determined blast of breath, she changed the subject. "Did Norman Pilkington come by today?"

Violet nodded. "I gave him a piece of my mind, told him the council is only doing its job and he needs to stop riling everyone up over this water tower thing. It looked like he had a bunch of names on that petition, though."

"Oh? He had forty-three when he came by the clinic."

"There were close to a hundred and fifty by the time he got here."

Millie sat back in her chair. "I had no idea he could rally that much support."

"I know. Haven't people *looked* at that water tower? If we let Little Norm paint it again, we could end up with fluorescent pink or pumpkin orange."

Imagine, a flamingo-pink water tower hovering above Main Street! With a low whistle, Millie shook her head.

Violet held up a finger and gave her the grin that always preceded a quote of which she was especially fond. "Whistling women and crowing hens always come to some bad end." The grin deepened. "That was one of my grandmother's favorites."

Millie's moan was interrupted by the whirring of the garage door opener. Rufus leaped off his cushion in the corner and began his nightly bark-o-rama while he ran to take up a position in front of the side door.

She glanced at the clock on the microwave. "What on earth is Albert doing home already? It's only four-twenty."

A few seconds later the door opened and a bouquet of colorful blossoms entered, followed by her husband. He'd brought her flowers? A wave of tenderness washed through her.

When he caught sight of them at the table, he halted and fixed a surprised stare on Violet. "Oh. Hullo."

With a glance toward Millie, she rose and bustled to the sink with her plate. "I'll come over in a bit and help you wash up." She hurried from the room.

"Don't bother," Millie called after her. "I'll call you later."

They heard the front door close, and Albert bent to give Rufus the customary pat on the head, which ended his noisy greeting. The dog trotted back to his cushion to resume his afternoon nap while an awkward silence settled in the kitchen.

Albert cleared his throat, and then thrust the flowers in her direction. "I got these on the way home. I wanted to get roses, but do you know how much roses cost?"

Ever the practical one, her Albert. Millie took the flowers, ignoring the red grocery store price sticker that announced they were discounted for quick sale. "These are beautiful." She buried her nose in them. No scent at all, but the bright colors made up for that. "Thank you."

He shuffled a shoe on the linoleum. "I'm sorry for last night."

Millie rose and covered the distance between them to throw her arms around his neck. "I'm sorry too. I hate arguing with you."

They stood for a moment, swaying with their embrace and releasing the leftover emotions from the night before. This was where she belonged, in her husband's arms holding a half-wilted bouquet of cheap flowers. In the grand scheme of things, did it matter which kitchen they stood in?

Well, yes, it did. A little. At least this kitchen did not have wheels.

Albert broke their embrace and, taking her by the hand, led her back to the table. "I want to discuss our retirement plans."

"Must we?" Millie lowered herself into the

chair he slid out for her. "I'd like to have a peaceful evening."

"We will," he said with a firm nod. He took the chair Violet had vacated. "I've thought about this all night and all day. You know our financial situation. We could afford to buy that house, but the renovation costs could wipe us out."

An excited tickle fluttered in her stomach. Was he actually considering her idea? "We can save money by doing a lot of them ourselves."

"Not plumbing and electrical work." His expression became dour. "And especially not roofing."

"We'd take bids, and go with the cheapest one."

He nodded. "That's exactly what we'd have to do. And if your bed and breakfast idea doesn't take off, I'll have to delay my retirement."

Millie could hardly believe her ears. Was that a *yes* she heard hovering in the midst of his dire predictions? Her pulse began a wild dance. "It will take off," she assured him with a certainty she felt in her bones.

His expression solemn, he caught her gaze. "Before you get too excited, I have several conditions that must be met."

Uh oh. Here it came. Of course there

would be conditions. Probably unachievable ones.

He held up a finger. "I insist on a full inspection, and if we find anything we can't afford to fix, the deal's off."

A reasonable request. She nodded. "Agreed."

A second finger shot into the air. "If we make an offer, it will be contingent on selling this house."

Again, not an unreasonable condition. She studied his face. Jaw set, chin jutted slightly forward in that stubborn pose she knew so well. He was about to drop a bomb. She gave a cautious nod to condition number two.

The third finger appeared. "And our offer will be five hundred thousand."

Ice water doused her enthusiasm. Of course Albert would make a lowball offer. She should never have told him what Violet said about the Updyke brothers' bottom dollar. They were sure to be insulted.

But this was far more ground than she'd expected to gain so quickly in the negotiations. Swallowing her doubts, she gave a regal nod. "Agreed."

At least she had the pleasure of watching his eyebrows shoot upward toward his thinning hairline.

■ ■ ■ ■

Al returned his toothbrush to the holder and switched off the bathroom light. He paused in the bedroom doorway. What a homey sight his wife made, propped up on pillows and leafing through a magazine, a faint smile hovering around those kissable lips. Far better than the rigid and frigid treatment he'd received last night.

Of course, he had not exactly acted like Prince Charming himself.

When he slid into bed, she put the magazine on her nightstand and scooted close to him, her head resting in the hollow of his shoulder. The faint, clean scent of the lilac soap she favored filled him with satisfaction, and he hugged her close.

"After we get the bed and breakfast established, we can still travel." Her lips moved against his pajama shirt as she spoke. "I'm sure camping in a travel trailer is much better than a tent."

"By the time we can afford to buy an RV, I'll be too old to drive it." He squeezed her tightly to acknowledge her concession. "But thank you."

"No, we'll get your RV," she insisted. "You'll see. Everything will work out."

He held his tongue. Actually, he was nearly positive that things *would* work out to his satisfaction. The odds of all three of his conditions being met were astronomical. Goose Creek was in decline — anyone could see that with a glance at all the empty buildings on Main Street. Who would want to move here? Mortgage rates were high, and the real estate market was sluggish. And besides, the Updykes would never accept his offer. Nobody was stupid enough to practically give away their family home.

Al turned off the light and settled himself comfortably beside his wife, prepared to dream of the RV he would buy when he retired.

MILLIE'S MINI VANILLA SCONE RECIPE

Scones
3 cups all-purpose flour
2/3 cups sugar
5 tsp baking powder
1/4 tsp salt
2 sticks cold unsalted butter
1 large egg
2 tsp vanilla extract
3/4 cup heavy cream (less 2 tsp)

Orange Vanilla Glaze
2 cups powdered sugar
Zest of 1 navel orange
3 Tbsp fresh orange juice
1/2 tsp vanilla
Approx 1/3 cup cream

Preheat the oven to 350°. Combine flour, sugar, baking powder, and salt, and sift. Cut in the butter until completely incorporated and crumbly. Beat the egg in a small bowl. Measure vanilla into a 3/4 measuring cup, then add cream to fill the cup. Stir the vanilla cream into the egg. Combine this with the flour, stirring just until a crumbly dough forms. Don't overmix.

Turn dough onto a floured surface and

press gently to form a long rectangle approximately 5 inches wide, 18 inches long, and 1 1/2 inches thick. Slice into smaller rectangles approximately 2 1/2 inches wide, and then cut each rectangle in half to form two small triangles. Place evenly on a baking sheet lined with parchment paper. Bake for 15 to 18 minutes. Remove them from the oven before they begin to brown. Cool for 15 minutes.

Whisk together the ingredients for the glaze until smooth. Dip one side of each scone into the glaze, and then cool until the glaze is set. Store in a sealed container.

CHAPTER EIGHT

Cell phone wedged between her cheek and shoulder, Millie tossed the car keys into her purse and grabbed her knitting bag off the passenger seat without missing a beat in her conversation with the church secretary. "I appreciate that, Doris. We're supposed to meet with Louise tonight to draw up the paperwork. Please ask everyone to pray that Albert will be reasonable about the asking price on our house. And that it sells quickly. And that the Updyke brothers are desperate enough to take our offer."

She paused in the act of opening the Volkswagen's door. Did that last request sound callous?

"Not that I want them to be desperate," she amended. "Only that I want them to accept our offer."

"I know what you mean." Doris's voice sounded even more shrill than usual this morning. Apparently she'd been making liberal use of that new espresso maker she'd bragged about at church on Sunday. "Don't worry. We'll assail the gates of heaven on your behalf."

Which was Doris's way of saying she would spread the word of the Richardsons' intent to buy the Updyke house and open Goose Creek's first bed and breakfast. Not only would an e-mail go out to the Woodview Community Church's prayer chain within five minutes, but no doubt the cellular airwaves above Goose Creek were already clogged with texts and phone calls discussing the irresistible news under the guise of a request for prayer. Church prayer chains were an efficient and effective means of communication that every small town employed in some form or other. The ladies of Goose Creek had perfected their technique to the point that a really juicy tidbit could spread from one side of town to the other within twenty-three minutes.

"Thanks, Doris." Millie opened her door as a car pulled into the animal clinic's parking lot. She glanced at the clock on her dashboard. Not yet eight o'clock, and Susan was already here. Doc never showed up before eight forty-five. "I've got to run," she told Doris. "I'll keep you posted."

She disconnected the call and dropped

the phone into her purse, and then exited the car to wait for Susan. The girl's face looked a little pale this morning above her starchy white lab coat. The poor thing probably hadn't slept a wink after the cold reception she'd received yesterday. Lizzie Forsythe, who had filled the role of afternoon receptionist since her husband opened the clinic, called last night to report that the rest of the day hadn't gone any better than the morning, with most everyone refusing to entrust their animals to any hands but Doc's.

She called a cheery greeting as Susan approached. "Good morning."

The younger woman eyed Millie's Volkswagen, her expression cautious. "Good morning. Your car's quite . . . pink, isn't it?"

"Yes, she is." Millie gave the Beetle's fender an affectionate pat. "My husband calls this color Pepto Pink."

"That fits," Susan agreed. She extended a finger to touch the tip of one of the curling black eyelashes that bordered the headlights, and then lifted a schooled expression to Millie. "Those add a girlie touch."

"That's why I got them. I'd get a pair for myself but I'm afraid they'd give my husband palpitations."

They walked together toward the clinic

and Millie stood aside while Susan unlocked the door. She had her own key, of course, but the poor thing deserved to have *some* sense of ownership over the clinic she was buying.

Inside, Millie bustled around the reception counter and stowed her purse and knitting in the bottom drawer of the filing cabinet. From the back room came the sound of high-pitched barking. Their only boarding customer was awake and eager to be released from his kennel.

She turned to find Susan standing somewhat awkwardly in the center of the room, clutching her purse and a slender briefcase and staring almost fearfully at the clinic door.

"Perhaps you could take Benji out for a walk while I get things set up here for the day," Millie suggested. Normally the tasks of walking and feeding the boarded pets fell to her, but the poor dear looked so forlorn. No doubt she'd appreciate the opportunity to take care of the playful Yorkie.

Her forehead cleared, the lines replaced by a purposeful expression. "Of course."

She disappeared through the door, and Millie called after her, "When he's done his business, you can feed him. He gets half a cup of the sweet potato formula."

"Okay," came the reply.

Millie smiled as she flipped on the computer. That should start the poor girl's day out right. It was a proven scientific fact that dogs were good for a person's blood pressure. Well, everyone except Albert's. The smile dimmed. Albert's blood pressure was the reason she'd brought Rufus home when his previous owner abandoned him on the front porch of the clinic. It had been a good plan, and would have worked, too, if only Rufus hadn't proven so stubborn in the area of potty training, and Albert hadn't proven so stubborn in the area of practically everything.

By the time Susan returned from caring for Benji, Millie had the reception desk arranged the way she liked it, with the stapler and paper clips in the corner to the left of the computer monitor and the cup full of pens up on the counter where clients could reach them. Every afternoon Lizzie insisted on putting those pens out of reach, reasoning that they were less likely to disappear if a client had to ask for one. But why on earth would a body go to the trouble of having their business name printed on ink pens if they didn't want to give them away? Pens were a marketing tool, far better than refrigerator magnets, and the more of them in circulation the better as far as she was concerned. When she opened her bed and breakfast, there would be cups full of pens with her logo on every retail counter in Goose Creek. Which reminded her of Violet's idea.

"My friend and I were brainstorming about ways to introduce you to the clients," she told Susan. "What about sending a postcard to everyone in our database offering a free introductory checkup?"

Creases carved across the girl's forehead. "Why would I want to do that?"

"Oh, you know." Millie adjusted the dog cookie jar a fraction. "Just to encourage people to come in and meet you."

"I plan to introduce myself during the regular course of business and let them see how I interact with their pets during an exam. My father thinks that will be the best way to prove I'm as competent as Dr. Forsythe."

Apparently the cool reception of yesterday's clients hadn't caused the girl sufficient concern yet. Of course she had no way of knowing how widely her comment about Arnold's toes had spread. And that bit of gossip wasn't even masked as a prayer request.

"Well, that's certainly one approach to

consider." Millie kept her voice clear of doubt. "But I know most of the people in this town, and I believe they'll be far more likely to come if they think they're getting a bargain."

Susan's frown deepened. "I can't afford to work for free. I'll have to start paying the bills as soon as the sale is finalized, and beginning next month I'll have loan payments."

"A discount then?" She smiled brightly. "Just on their first visit. I think it will go a long way toward showing people you're sincere."

Her head cocked sideways. "Sincere about what?"

"About your concern for their pets. Doc is well known, and everyone loves him. I'm sure when they get to know you they'll love you too. But sometimes a person has to take the first step toward friendship." She paused. How to put this delicately? "Especially when they have something to overcome."

"Something to overcome?" Millie remained silent, and after a moment, realization dawned in Susan's gray eyes. "Is this about that polydactyl cat?"

Millie awarded her an apologetic smile. "Delores has a lot of friends."

She groaned and sagged against the wall, her hands covering her face. "I didn't say I wanted to cut his toe off."

"I know, and I'll correct anyone who says otherwise. In the meantime, some sort of goodwill gesture might be in order."

An expression of abject dismay overtook the girl's features, and sympathy twinged strongly in Millie. Poor Susan. She looked so young, so vulnerable and . . . well, it must be said. So clueless.

Susan gave a resigned nod. "I'll talk it over with Daddy tonight and let you know to-morrow."

Though Millie was perfectly willing to talk the matter over with her right then, she confined her reaction to an agreeable nod. Let the girl talk with her father. If the man had any brains at all, he would see the sense of the suggestion.

When Al turned the corner onto Mulberry Avenue and spied the red Camry in his driveway, his mood soured. The realtor was here already. Though Millie informed him earlier that Louise would be here tonight to draw up the paperwork, he assumed he'd at least be allowed the pleasure of dinner before having to deal with her. Talking about real estate on an empty stomach would no doubt upset his digestion. And besides, her car was blocking his side of the garage, which meant he had to park on the street.

He did so, grumbling while he retrieved his wallet from the center console. If there was one thing he detested more than squirrels, it was paperwork. No doubt he would be faced with a ton of it, since they had two houses to deal with. And for what? The entire evening would be a waste of time. There was no way the Updyke brothers would accept such a pathetic offer. And even if they did, there was even less chance that their house would sell. Not in this economy, and certainly not for the price he intended to ask.

Slamming the car door behind him, he made his way down the walkway, admiring the new growth on his Camellias. He scanned the neat squares of grass on either side of the walkway. Louise would probably want to install a sign. Oh, how he would hate coming home every day and seeing the symmetry of his front yard disturbed with an ugly For Sale sign. Plus, he'd have to mow around it.

With another ill-tempered grumble he entered the house through the front door. Rufus came charging out of the kitchen indulging in his nightly barking fit. Tonight his bark held an unaccustomed intensity, no doubt fussing because Al didn't enter through the garage. Rufus disliked the interruption of their regular routine as much as Al.

"Yes, I know. I'm not happy about it either," Al told him, giving his head an extra couple of pats to compensate.

Millie's voice called from the kitchen. "We're in here, honey."

He found them at the kitchen table, a neat stack of papers resting ominously between them. Louise, who had an ink pen protruding from a bun of blonde hair at the back of her head, set her iced tea on the placemat and rose from her chair.

"Nice to see you again, Al."

He endured a handshake and stooped to brush a kiss on Millie's upturned cheek while the realtor settled herself.

"Would you like some ice water?" his wife asked.

Feeling deprived, he eyed their glasses. Millie could drink tea all day without being affected in the slightest. If he drank tea this late, he'd be up all night.

"No, thanks." He joined them at the table, folded his hands, and turned an expectant look on Louise. "Millie told you the conditions of our offer?"

She was cool, he'd give her that. Her smile appeared completely genuine as she patted the stack of papers. "I've got everything written up, ready for your signature."

He nodded. Maybe this wouldn't take all night after all.

"I've given Louise a tour of the house," Millie told him, "and she's already done some research to help us figure out what we should ask."

"You have a beautiful home here, Al."

"Thank you." He pasted on a chilly smile and avoided looking in Millie's direction. "We've been very happy here."

"There weren't many comps to pull." Her pink manicured fingers flipped over the top three papers and she handed them to him. "The market has been in a slump for a while. Now, if you were in Lexington we'd probably see a lot of action. As it is . . ." She shrugged.

Of the three homes she identified as comparable, he was familiar with two.

"Hardister's place?" He scanned the page. "It's half the size of ours. Only two bedrooms and one bathroom."

"We take that into consideration when we put a value on a house." She picked up her glass. "It sold for sixty-five thousand, which is considerably less than yours is worth."

"You bet it is." He glanced at the second paper. He knew something about this house too. "I heard the Kramers had to spend close to ten thousand to make the house livable before they could move in."

"They redecorated the kitchen and renovated the master bathroom." Millie gave him a scolding stare. "Both needed to be done, but the home was perfectly livable when they bought it."

"That's a three-two like yours," Louise put in. "One forty-five was a good price for that property."

"It's also ten years older than ours." Al picked up the third sheet and examined the address. "This is that place over on Cottage Grove Drive. I thought that was still for sale."

"It is, technically, but it's under contract. A retired couple from Danville is buying it for one sixty-two."

"It has almost a thousand square feet less than this place."

"But it's on a half-acre corner lot," she pointed out. "With a privacy fence."

Al tossed the paper on the table and it fluttered to rest on the others. From the corner of his eye he saw Millie's lips tighten. He folded his hands again and fixed a look on the realtor. "What do you think our asking price should be?"

"After looking at these, and analyzing the homes in the area that have been on the market but haven't sold, I think a good starting place is one seventy-two. That leaves a bit of room for negotiating, and we may have to drop the price if we don't get enough activity within the first couple of weeks, but —"

"One eighty-five."

Millie sucked in a noisy breath, and the first crack in the realtor's professional mask appeared. Her penciled-on eyebrows arched. She folded her hands in an imitation of his. "I think that's an overly optimistic price, Al."

"I agree," added Millie, her tone tinged with anger.

"We paid one thirty-five seventeen years ago," he replied calmly. "Surely in seventeen years the value of real estate has increased."

Louise matched his tone. "I'm sure it has, but not thirty-seven percent. Certainly not in Goose Creek."

Al was mildly impressed that she'd done the calculation in her head so quickly. "I'm not going to give this house away. My price is one eighty-five."

Millie folded her arms across her chest and fixed him with a glare. "You're being purposefully obstinate."

He shook his head. "I've done a careful examination of our financial resources, and made some assumptions about the cost of renovations on that monstr" — he changed the word — "on the Updyke house, and that's what we need in order to make this work."

"I doubt thirteen thousand dollars will make that much of a difference in your calculations."

"Thirteen thousand dollars won't begin to cover the cost of a new roof," he shot back. "If we're going to buy a house that old we'll need every cent we can scrape together."

"All right." Louise cut smoothly into their conversation before it escalated into a full-fledged argument. "One eighty-five it is. We'll see what kind of activity that generates."

She flipped over another few pages, extracted the pen from her hair, and wrote the figure in the appropriate place. "Now let's go over the offer document. I want to make sure you don't have any questions before you sign."

Feeling as though he had won a major victory, Al endured the next half hour and listened more or less attentively while the realtor explained each paragraph of both contracts. He stole the occasional glance at Millie, who eventually stopped fuming, though the hard set to her lips did not soften. They signed their names a dozen times and their initials two dozen more before the ordeal was over.

Finally Louise shuffled the whole mess into a neat stack and shoved it into her briefcase. "I'll make copies and drop them by tomorrow."

"What do you think the Updykes will say to our offer?" Apprehension flooded Millie's question.

Louise gave an elegant shrug as she rose. "We'll know in a few days. I'll call you the minute I have their response."

Al stood and shook her hand, but remained in the kitchen while Millie walked her to the front door. Hushed whispers drifted back to him, but he couldn't make out the words. No doubt comparing notes on what a stubborn old poop he was. That was okay. He'd put his foot down, stuck to his guns, and gotten his way. A successful evening by his reckoning, though no doubt his wife would disagree. Perhaps a peace offering would be in order.

When she returned, he spoke first. "How about we go out to dinner? It's going to be a mild night. We could walk down to the Bistro."

Her favorite of the town's three restaurants, though a little pricier than he liked. She studied him with a shrewd, narrow-eyed stare, obviously not fooled one bit. Not that he'd expected her to be. His Millie was too sharp for that.

But she was also a peace-loving woman. Her expression cleared and she shook her head. "There's no sense spending the money when we have so many leftovers. Let's stay in."

That suited Al just fine. He left her bustling around the kitchen, pulling dishes out of the fridge, and headed to the bedroom to change out of his work clothes. As he passed the front window, he paused to watch Louise pound a huge, ugly For Sale sign in his front yard. It wouldn't be there long, of that he was confident.

Al had just settled into his recliner after a delicious dinner of leftover anniversary roast beef when the phone rang. Rufus leaped up to sound an alarm, just in case they had not noticed. He and Millie eyed each other.

"It's your turn," Al told her.

"No it's not."

"Yes it is. I got it when Doug called the

other day."

With a resigned sigh Millie set her knitting in the basket and heaved herself out of her chair. Rufus trotted after her into the kitchen. Al sat back and returned his attention to the TV screen. Someday he would install a telephone line here in the family room. They had the cordless in the kitchen but never remembered to bring it with them when they settled in front of the television for the night.

A squeal from the kitchen brought him upright in his recliner. Millie came running into the room, the phone clutched in her hand, eyes dancing.

"They took it! They took our offer!"

"Huh?" Numbness stole over Al's brain like fog creeping over a river. He was vaguely aware that somewhere in the distance dark clouds gathered on the horizon of his future. His carefully laid plan, designed to ensure a peaceful retirement spent traveling the country, had unexpectedly hit a roadblock on the first step.

"They accepted five hundred thousand dollars?" He could barely choke the words out. Surely the Updyke brothers were not *that* desperate for money.

Millie waved an impatient hand in his direction and then stuck a finger in her left ear, focusing on whatever she was hearing through the telephone. "Okay. Yes, of course. I think that's perfectly reasonable. I'm sure Al won't mind agreeing to that."

"Mind agreeing to what?"

Millie unplugged her ear and placed a hand over the receiver. "They want to add a kick-out clause. I'll explain in a minute."

A kick-out clause? Did that mean they were reserving the right to come down at a future date and kick them out of the house? No, surely not. Al perched on the edge of the recliner and watched Millie's face as she listened.

"Are you serious? No other conditions?" A pause. "All right. I'll go over that with Al, and we'll drop by tomorrow when he gets off of work to sign the papers." She giggled — actually giggled — and said, "Thank you so much, Louise. I can't tell you how excited I am!" She punched the disconnect button and launched herself across the room. In the next moment Al found his lap full of Millie. "We're going to buy the Updyke house! Oh Al, I can hardly believe it."

Al could hardly believe it himself. "What's a kick-out clause?"

"If someone comes along with a better offer before we close on the house, the Updykes have the right to accept that offer instead of ours." A frown tugged at the corners of Millie's mouth. "Louise says she doesn't think that's likely, because no one else has looked at the property at all. But the house just went on the market. Word may spread, and our offer is awfully low."

One ray of hope in an otherwise gloomy situation, as far as Al was concerned. "We still have to sell this house," he warned. "And don't forget my condition about the inspection."

"I know." She threw her arms around his neck for another squeeze. "But if it's meant to be, everything will fall into place. And I believe it's meant to be." Then she bounced out of his lap and began punching numbers into the handset as she dashed from the room. "I've got to call Violet. She won't believe it."

The sound of enthusiastic chatter drifted through the kitchen doorway. Alone in the family room, Al stared morosely at his slippers. He was not ready to concede victory yet. He had placed several high hurdles on the path before them, and he would not lower a single one. If Millie thought he'd been stubborn as a post before, she was about to meet an unyielding force the likes of which she'd never encountered in her heretofore indulgent husband. No budging, not even an inch.

Still, he couldn't shake the feeling that he had lost important ground in this battle of wills.

CHAPTER NINE

"I'm going on vacation," announced Doc Forsythe. "Leaving tomorrow."

The past week has been dismal enough to dampen Susan's enthusiasm about her new business. In fact, she almost backed out of the deal entirely two days ago while standing in the loan officer's office with a pen poised above the empty signature line, ready to sign the papers. But Daddy's confidence bolstered her, and now the loan was a done deal. The money was in the process of being transferred, and there was nothing she could do about it.

She clutched the edge of the reception desk and tried to school the panic out of her voice. "What do you mean you're going on vacation? You can't desert me."

"Of course I can." The older man gave her a fatherly pat on the shoulder. "You are doing just fine."

Seated in her rolling chair behind the

reception counter, Millie remained silent, but her eyebrows arched at the remark.

"Fine?" Susan's voice squeaked. "I've examined exactly three animals in the past ten days. And one of those was a drop-off. When the owner picked him up she was furious that you hadn't completed the examination." She whirled toward Millie for verification. "Isn't that right?"

The ever-honest receptionist conceded with a reluctant nod. "She wasn't thrilled."

"Creekers are a stubborn bunch," Doc agreed. "But don't worry. You'll grow on them."

"I don't think I'll grow on them by tomorrow."

Doc's expression became serious. "My leaving is the best thing that can happen to you at this point. When I'm gone they'll have nobody else to turn to. They'll have to come here, and that's your chance to prove yourself."

"You don't think they'll start taking their pets out of town?" A hint of desperation crept into the question.

The older man toyed with a new growth of gray hair on his upper lip. "Some of them probably will." Her spirits sank toward the floor. "But emergencies are bound to happen. Animals get sick, and their owners will call here out of habit. If you're the only doctor available . . ." He shrugged.

"They'll be stuck with me." She tried not to sound like a sullen child.

"They'll be happy to have a competent, qualified veterinarian right in town," he corrected.

Before she could voice her next question, Millie did. "Why the short notice? Surely you didn't just decide to pick up and go on vacation last night."

"Why not?" A wide grin settled on his face. "We're retiring. We're learning to be spontaneous. Lizzie found a good deal on a last-minute rental in Orlando and made some calls. We're going to check out a few retirement communities while we're down there, including the one my mother lives in."

"Who'll be covering afternoons at the desk?" Millie placed her hands on the reception counter in a possessive manner.

"Lizzie's going to contact Hazel and Carol this morning. If you're interested in picking up a few extra hours, you can have as many as you want."

She looked thoughtful a moment. "Actually, I could use the extra money for my renovation fund. Just for a week, though. I don't want a full-time job."

"Fine. Give Lizzie a call." He turned a kind look toward Susan. "I suggest you start interviewing for a replacement immediately. When we return my wife wants to cut her hours way back so she can start packing for the move. The house is going on the market tonight."

A lump lodged in Susan's throat, and she managed a nod.

"Good luck with that," Millie said darkly, a frown on her customarily cheerful face. "We haven't had a single looker, and it's been over a week."

Susan's mind whirled. Interview for a new receptionist? She didn't even know if she could afford to continue paying Millie her part-time wage.

"And of course we'll board Ajax here." Doc gave her a pleasant pat on the arm. "See, there's your first solo customer."

"Ajax?"

"A bull terrier mix Lizzie and I adopted a few years ago," he said. "A bit on the rambunctious side, but smart as a whip. You'll love him."

The front door opened, and the first client of the day entered.

"Francine, you're a sight for sore eyes this fine morning." Doc's booming voice filled the small reception area. He laid an arm across Susan's shoulders and pulled her forward. "Allow me to introduce Dr. Jeffries. Susan, meet Francine Ryan and one of our many six-toed patients, Smokey."

The middle-aged woman clutched a gray cat close to her chest and eyed Susan with alarm. "I heard you were retiring," she told Doc without removing a horrified stare from Susan, "but I hoped it was a rumor. I don't trust Smokey to —"

"Nonsense." Doc cut her off and deftly removed the cat from her arms. "I hand-picked Dr. Jeffries myself. Smokey will love her."

He shoved the feline at Susan and guided a protesting Mrs. Ryan toward the clinic door. Well, that was one way to get her accepted — by brute force. But what would happen tomorrow, when Doc Forsythe headed south to Florida? She had to do something to put herself in the good graces of the local pet owners. Otherwise, her business would fail before the first loan payment was due.

Holding the warm, purring body carefully, she trailed after Doc while compiling a mental list of compliments, most involving the creature's unusual sixth digit. At the clinic doorway, she turned to Millie.

"You know those postcards you mentioned

last week?" Daddy hadn't thought a promotion of that sort necessary, but he was down in Paducah, hours and miles away. He didn't realize how desperate the situation was here in Goose Creek. "I can't do free, but what about fifty percent off the first checkup?"

Millie gave an approving nod. "I think that should attract some attention."

"How quickly can we have some printed?"

A dimple appeared in each cheek. "Leave it to me. I know a guy."

On Wednesday morning Millie whipped the Beetle into the parking lot to find Susan's car already there. Goodness, what a dedicated young woman. Gathering her knitting bag, purse, and a large envelope, she exited the Beetle, noting as she passed Susan's car that the windshield held an unbroken layer of foggy moisture. How long had the girl been there? She must have arrived in the wee hours of the morning for the dew to settle like that.

Juggling her bags to unlock the front door, Millie stepped inside. Light shone from the cracks around the clinic door, but the waiting room remained dark.

"Hello?" She directed her voice toward the back as she rounded the reception counter and stowed her belongings in the file cabinet.

The door swung open and Susan appeared, a steaming coffee mug in one hand. A brief almost-smile flashed onto her solemn face and she gave a quiet, "Good morning."

"And I thought *I* was an early riser," Millie said as she slid the drawer shut. "You must have gotten here hours before sunup."

"Well, uh." The girl didn't quite meet her gaze. "Yes."

Millie examined her more closely. Her straight hair, which was a nondescript dark blond, hung damply to the shoulders of a crisp white lab coat with *Dr. S. Jeffries* embroidered above the breast pocket. In terms of makeup, the girl typically wore little more than pale pink lipstick and a bit of mascara — Millie had thought several times that a touch of color on her cheeks would emphasize her eyes — but today she wore none at all. When she stepped near, the scent of soap clung strongly to her.

The reason hit Millie in a flash. "Did you spend the night here?"

A guilty flush crept over Susan's cheeks. "Well, yes. Doc said he was going to bring Ajax late last night and kennel him so they could leave first thing this morning. I wanted to be here for a personal introduction. So while I was waiting, it occurred to me that it's a waste of money to pay for a hotel when there's plenty of room in the back office, and a hand-held sprayer in the grooming sink, and a microwave and coffeepot. So I drove to Lexington and got my lizard and —"

"Your lizard?" Millie interrupted, trying to banish the image of the girl washing up in the dog washing sink.

Susan nodded. "His name is Puff. I checked out of the Holiday Inn and picked up a camping cot and sleeping bag at Walmart on the way back." She smoothed a damp lock of hair behind her ear and gave Millie a slightly defensive look. "It's very comfortable."

Millie stared at the girl. Were her finances so desperate, then? How could she afford to buy the clinic if she couldn't even pay for a hotel room?

Though she really should discuss this with Albert before offering, Millie couldn't stop herself. "My husband and I have two spare bedrooms, and we'd be happy to have you stay with us until you find something in town."

But Susan shook her head. "I'll be fine here. Actually, I prefer it. I can work on the files as late as I want and keep an eye on the boarded animals." Her gaze circled the room, and a slight smile played around the corners of her lips. "Besides, it makes me feel more like it's really mine, you know?"

In an odd way, Millie did. "At least accept an invitation to dinner every few days." She cocked her head and added, "And you might find the occasional use of my guest bathroom's shower preferable to dousing yourself in the dog bath every day."

To her surprise, the girl laughed, the first time Millie had heard her make the sound. "I can't argue with that. Thank you."

"Oh, before I forget." Millie picked up the large envelope she'd brought from home and pulled out a sheet of paper. "What do you think of this? My husband drew it up last night." She handed over a copy of Albert's draft postcard and watched Susan's face light up.

"This is really good." She held the paper at arm's length and tilted her head. "I like the font he used for *Introducing Dr. Susan Jeffries.* And those little scissors around the dotted line make it look like a real coupon."

"My Albert is so talented." Millie didn't bother to filter the pride from her voice. "I counted our client list, and figure if we print 250 we'll have enough to send one to everyone and have some leftover to set out on the counter in case people forget theirs. And I know Lucy Cardwell will let us put some by the cash register down at the drug store."

"Good thinking. I'm going to fax this to Daddy and make sure he approves."

The comment struck Millie as odd. Of course it was perfectly fine to ask for advice from someone you respect. Their own children, who were only a few years older than Susan, often called to discuss their decisions with Albert and her. But the idea of a grown woman, a business owner, having to get *approval* from her father?

Of course, her father did cosign the loan. Millie had overheard her discussing that fact with Doc last week. Still, wouldn't the man encourage her to make her own business decisions?

She stood aside while Susan headed toward the fax machine resting on the corner of the reception counter, behind the dog cookie jar. "Is your father a businessman?"

"Oh yes. He's a bank vice president down in Paducah." Susan dropped the paper into the machine and punched a series of numbers on the front panel. "He's got great instincts about business and finances and practically everything else. I never make a move without consulting Daddy first."

Well, that made sense. While the fax machine whirred and buzzed to scan Albert's paper, Millie booted up the computer for the day. She replaced the pen cup with a smile. In Lizzie's absence it would stay in place for a full week.

Within two minutes, Susan's cell phone rang. She extracted it from her lab coat pocket.

"Good morning, Daddy," she answered in a cheerful tone.

Millie heard the drone of a deep male voice.

"It's a postcard with an introductory offer to generate business. My morning receptionist's husband designed it. Doesn't it look great?"

The man's tone did not change, but Susan's expression did. Her smile faded and, with a quick glance at Millie, she headed toward her office.

"I know we did," her voice drifted back to Millie in the seconds before the door swung shut, "but if you could see . . ."

Eavesdropping became impossible. The conversation continued in the back office, Susan's voice barely audible above the whirr of the printer as it spit out the day's appointment schedule. Millie glanced over the list, noting the names that were likely to cancel their appointments when they learned of Doc's absence. Unfortunately there were quite a few. Ah, but Mrs. Olsen was scheduled to bring her poodle, Tiny, in at ten for a checkup. Surely that sweet, elderly soul would take pity on poor Susan and allow her to conduct the exam. In fact, Millie might just make a call —

The clinic door opened and Susan stood in the doorway, her face unreadable.

"Please tell your husband how much I appreciate his work," she said in a carefully even tone. "On second thought, I think I'll hold off on the discount offer for the time being."

Though Millie didn't know the girl well, the rapid convulsions of her throat spoke of tears being swallowed back.

"If you change your mind, I can have them printed and mailed within a couple of days."

With another swallow, Susan nodded and disappeared back into the office. Millie stared at the door thoughtfully. The poor child. In many ways she seemed very young, regardless of her education and accomplishments.

Millie's glance fell on the fax machine and a hard knot settled in the pit of her stomach.

How awful of her to take a dislike to a man she'd never even met.

CHAPTER TEN

The Goose Creek City Hall was situated in the ancient brick building that used to house the jail, back in the days when the town was responsible for dispensing justice on its own. Al figured the building was old even when the Updyke house had been built. The cells in the back of the building had been renovated into a conference room, and the second floor contained offices for the Mayor and Sally Bright, his secretary.

The City Council met the first and third Thursdays of every month. Normally these meetings were attended only by the six Council members. Though the public was invited to attend any meeting, no one ever bothered. Al held the general impression that the meetings were spent going over complaint letters involving residents who failed to clean up after their pets or had noisy neighbors.

But tonight's meeting was different. After

supper, Al donned his jacket, kissed Millie's cheek, and headed for Main Street. He intended to maintain a cautious stance of noncommittal in the case of the water tower painting contract, but with the remote possibility that he might one day become a business owner in Goose Creek, he felt it prudent to at least stay advised on the issue.

Apparently he was not the only one. When he turned the corner to Main Street he spied a crowd on the sidewalk outside of City Hall. Dividing lines had definitely been drawn. To one side stood a small group clustered around Norman Pilkington, who was expressing his opinion loudly and with much waving of his hands in the air. Instead of his usual worn T-shirt, he'd donned a blue button-up this evening and tucked it into a pair of relatively clean baggy denims. Al scanned the faces around him. No sign of Little Norm. Odd, since he stood to benefit the most if his father's petition was successful tonight.

A few feet away stood a slightly larger crowd with apparently no leader, since they stared off into space, shuffled on their feet, and appeared to put forth an effort not to meet anyone's eye. Al spied a few familiar faces. Pete Lawson, the Cardwells, and

Miles Stockton. Since they had all been vocal in their support of the Council putting the painting project out to bid, Al recognized that group as Norman's opposition.

A third group stood a noticeable distance away. He knew even more of these people, and gravitated toward them. He slid into place beside Bill Zigler, a friend from church with whom he had spoken the night before. Bill and the others in this group had decided to maintain a neutral stance in the painting contract dispute.

"Quite a crowd tonight," commented Bill.

Al nodded. "Didn't expect as many."

"Nobody wants to miss a good fight," put in Fred Rightmeier from behind.

"Let's hope it doesn't come to that," Al said over his shoulder.

"From the looks of those guys over there," Bill nodded his head toward Norman's group, "I have a feeling it may."

A movement across the street drew their attention. Diane Hudson and Phyllis Bozart, both Council members, crossed to the center of the street and hesitated on the railroad tracks, their gazes sweeping the crowd. Al detected caution in both ladies' stances. Diane clutched her handbag to her chest with both hands while Phyllis hugged herself tightly across her middle. The crowd noticed them.

"Hey, there's two of 'em now," shouted Norman. "How you gonna vote tonight?"

The ladies exchanged glances and Diane answered. "We have several issues on the agenda tonight."

An obvious stalling technique, and one that did not find favor with the crowd, who grumbled.

Norman held a spiral notebook above his head and shook it. "I got yer issue right here."

The ladies were saved from answering when the City Hall door opened from the inside. Mayor Selbo appeared on the doorstep, his gaze fixed on the pair. "Ladies, come on in. The rest of the Council is inside and we're about ready to start."

As they made their way across the street people began to press toward the door.

Jerry held up his hands. "Were not quite ready to let the public in yet."

Norman marched up to him. "This here's a public meeting, ain't it? We aim to come in and say our piece."

"And you will have the opportunity, but first the Council has some things to discuss in private."

"Whaddya mean, private?" Norman turned toward the crowd. "They ain't allowed to do that, are they?"

Jerry raised his voice to be heard above the answering grumbles. "If you check the Council's charter you'll discover that we are within our rights to close some meetings to the public. Now, we don't intend to do that tonight. We want to hear what you have to say. But first we need to establish some guidelines among the Council members." The two nervous Council women arrived at the door and Jerry ushered them inside. "I'll let you know when it's your turn to speak. I promise I won't leave you out here long."

He closed the door behind him, and a murmur arose from the people on the sidewalk. How in the world Jerry remained so calm Al couldn't imagine. His estimation of the mayor rose a few notches.

Lucy turned. "Any luck selling your house yet?"

"None at all." He tried not to sound cheerful. "Haven't had a single showing."

Leonard, whose shoulders seemed even more stooped without his customary white pharmacy coat, sucked in his cheeks. The gesture made his narrow face appear even more gaunt than usual. "Tough market."

Several heads nodded agreement, but Lucy awarded Al with a bright smile. "I wouldn't worry. As I told Millie, things will work out for the best. They always do."

Since that's what Al was counting on, he nodded agreement.

Fifteen minutes passed, and those waiting outside fidgeted. A note of irritation infected the mumbling, and Al's patience began to evaporate. Maybe he'd just head on home after all. No doubt Millie would hear all about the meeting tomorrow and would report every detail. He opened his mouth to bid farewell to Bill, but snapped it shut when the door opened.

The mayor appeared once again. "Thank you for your patience. Tonight's City Council meeting is now declared open to the public." He gave an apologetic grimace. "I'm afraid there's not much room in here. Hope you don't mind getting friendly with your neighbors."

A few in the center group chuckled as everyone pressed forward. Norman, clutching his notebook in a fist, pushed to the front. Al found himself swept along with the crowd.

Instead of the back conference room, the Council members had arranged their chairs behind a couple of long folding tables on the far side of the main entry room. Al saw the wisdom of that immediately. This room was bigger, though not nearly large enough to hold the number of people waiting outside. There were no chairs, so he found himself squashed shoulder-to-shoulder between Bill and Jacob Pulliam, squarely behind Leonard. From this vantage point he could see Gary Vandergrift on the far left of the line of Council members, half of Aaron Southworth, and on the opposite end he had a good view of Lynn Bowers. Beside her, perched on the end, sat Sally with her pen poised above a legal pad. Someone pressed him from behind, and he dug his heels in to keep from having his nose shoved into Lenoard's back.

Jerry skirted the table and took his chair in the center, completely hidden from view behind Leonard's sweater-draped body. "Sorry about the wait, folks. Thanks for your cooperation."

Someone on the far side of the room shouted toward the mayor. "What'd y'all talk about while we was outside?"

"Mostly we were rearranging the furniture." Al heard a laugh in Jerry's voice, which was answered by several in the audience. "And we called the meeting to order and checked a few things in our charter. You can read about it in the minutes, if you're interested."

Norman, who stood front and center of

the onlookers, brandished his notebook in the air above his balding head. "I got a petition here that says —"

"Hold on there, Norman." Jerry's voice, polite but stern enough to be commanding, cut the man off. "This is an official meeting of the Goose Creek City Council. We have a published agenda, and we're obliged to follow it. I'll let you know when it's your turn to speak."

From his vantage point, Al watched Norman's mouth snap shut in profile and his cheeks bulge. He jerked a nod.

"First order of business," continued Jerry, "is a report from Kentucky American Water. Lynn, I believe you have that."

Lynn bent over a paper in front of her, her bangs falling forward. "I do. They report that the fence surrounding the meter pit on Junior Watson's farm has been built and is now secure from livestock. Apparently it took longer than anticipated because the workmen had to be dispatched multiple times."

A voice from the back of the room piped up. "I reckon so. I wouldn't go in that pasture either, with Junior refusin' to round up that ornery bull of his. A feller could end up on the wrong side of a beefsteak dinner that'a'way."

146

Several people snickered, and Lynn's lips twitched before she continued. "On a positive note, they say they've obtained the necessary easements to run a twelve-inch line to Goose Creek that ought to help the supply to several parts of town." She pushed the paper forward on the table's surface.

"That's fine," said Jerry. "Any discussion on that issue?"

Gary and Aaron, and presumably the rest of the Council, shook their heads.

"Good. We'll count that one closed. Next on the agenda is the complaint about Paul Simpson's back deck. Aaron, you have that one, don't you?"

The sheet of paper Aaron picked up trembled visibly. Al felt a wave of sympathy for the reclusive man. He'd won his appointment to the Council last year when his mother, feeling he needed a shove into the public eye if he was to catch the attention of a suitable wife, asked her ladies' group to write him in as a candidate.

He cleared his throat. "Last year the Council approved an encroachment permit for Mr. Simpson to install pavers leading through his yard and out to the street to aid in water drainage. Turns out Mr. Simpson poured concrete instead of pavers. The complaint came from one of his neighbors."

"Somebody ought to tell old lady Emerson to mind her own business," came a female voice from somewhere to Al's right.

Jerry ignored the comment. "What'd you find out, Aaron?"

The man answered in a monotone, reading his response from the wavering paper. "Jim Maybrier and I inspected the path during a heavy rain. In Mr. Maybrier's professional opinion, there is no difference in the way water runs off from concrete as opposed to the originally proposed pavers. I also checked the ordinance and discovered that there is no requirement for a citizen to file an amended request for a permit when the method or materials change, as long as the original stated intent is achieved. Therefore I move that the issue be dismissed without further action." He set the paper down and sank against the back of his chair.

"I second," piped up Phyllis.

"Any discussion?" asked Jerry. Silence. "Then all in favor?"

The hands that Al could see all lifted.

"Let the minutes reflect that the motion is passed unanimously."

A loud sigh sounded from somewhere behind Al. He cranked his head and caught sight of Paul Simpson mopping his brow with a red handkerchief.

"And now to the issue that has brought us all here tonight." Al detected a note of resignation in Jerry's voice. "Next on the agenda is the painting of Goose Creek's water tower." Before anyone could say a word he continued. "First we will review the discussions from our previous meetings, and then we will open the floor."

"What previous meetings? Shouldn't we have been involved in those?" The question came from Woody Edwards, who stood beside Norman.

"The primary discussion occurred at our last meeting," answered Gary. "Nobody attended that one, or any other Council meeting in the past six months."

"That's 'cause they're so boring," piped up someone from behind.

Jerry's ever-patient voice rose over the answering laughter. "The minutes of our meetings are a matter of public record. If you want to know what happened at the last meeting, give us a call at the office and Sally will be happy to email you a copy. But to make sure everyone's up to speed, let me recap."

Al edged sideways, though his shoulder pressed uncomfortably against Jacob's, and angled his head so he could see most of Jerry's face. Cool as a cucumber, though was that a sheen of sweat on his forehead? Might be the temperature, though. With all these people in the room, Al was starting to feel a bit warm himself. He'd shrug out of his jacket if he had the room. What would the fire marshal say about the capacity of this room to hold a crowd this size?

The mayor put on a pair of reading glasses and scanned a document on the table in front of him. "Last month it was brought to the Council's attention by a member of the community that the water tower's peeling paint was unsightly and cast the town in a bad light to visitors."

"That's true enough," agreed Miles from the audience.

Jerry glanced up over the top of the glasses, and then continued. "The Council discussed the complaint and agreed that it had merit, and unanimously approved the expenditure of having the tower painted. We also agreed that the job should be completed before our annual Fall Festival, in order to maximize the town's appeal to outsiders."

He paused. Tension mounted among the onlookers as they waited for him to continue. The hair on Al's arms actually prickled beneath his jacket.

The mayor cleared his throat and kept his gaze fixed on the document. "There was a concern expressed by a member of the Council" — he looked briefly up — "that the existing paint job had not lasted nearly as long as should be expected."

"Been havin' some nasty weather these past few years," said Norman in a loud and defensive tone. A few murmurs of agreement answered him, but most everyone stayed silent.

"The rest of the Council agreed. We also discussed the Council's obligation to manage public funds in a conscientious manner."

Al considered that last remark. In other words, they'd probably talked about what a waste of money it had been to pay Little Norm for substandard workmanship. Not to mention the disturbing color.

"Managing public funds is what we're talkin' about," said Norman.

Now Jerry showed the first signs of impatience. He removed his glasses and leveled a stare on Norman. "We haven't opened the floor for discussion yet. You'll have the opportunity to speak, so please save your comments until that time."

Nicely handled. Good for him.

Norman cast an outraged glance to those in his immediate vicinity, but held his tongue.

The glasses were put back on. "After much consideration, the council agreed that the most fiscally responsible action was to publish a Request for Bid. I undertook the task of drafting the RFB, which I have circulated and hope you've all had time to read." He paused, and the Council members Al could see all nodded. Sally scribbled on her legal pad.

"Did anyone have any questions?" He looked up. "Anyone *on the Council,* I mean."

"I do," said Diane. "In section 12.a you said the bids have to be submitted by April twentieth. That gives prospective painters less than two weeks. Is that enough time?"

Gary answered. "It'll have to be. Summer is a busy time for painters, so we'll probably run into scheduling conflicts. We need to give them as much time as possible to finish the job by the Festival at the beginning of September."

Norman apparently couldn't let that comment pass. "Bull flookies. Don't take hardly no time a'tall to slap some paint on a water tower."

Al exchanged a glance with Bill. Obviously, that was the problem last time. Little Norm completed the job quickly, and the town had suffered for it ever since.

The mayor ignored the outburst. "I agree,

Gary. Sally has assembled a list of potential painters, so in addition to filing the RFB publicly, we'll also be sending a dozen or so directly. They'll know about it within a couple of days, which should give them plenty of time to respond. Any other questions?" Jerry's glance slid up and down both sides of the table. When no one answered, his chest inflated slowly. He stood, removed his glasses, and gazed at the onlookers. "Okay then. Let's open this issue for discussion." Before anyone could speak, he held up a hand. "This will be conducted in an orderly fashion. If you have something to say, please make your way to the front row and raise your hand. I will call on each of you in turn. We don't have a microphone, so speak loudly enough to be heard by everyone. First please state your name so Sally can record it in the minutes."

Norman, already on the front row, shot his hand in the air. A few other hands also rose, and the crowd began to shuffle as some attempted to make their way forward. Al took the opportunity to edge sideways to take up a position behind Lucy. From that vantage point he could see the entire Council over the top of her head.

Jerry pointed with his glasses at Norman, and then lowered himself to his seat.

Norman spoke to Sally, his gravelly voice loud. "Name's Norman Pilkington, Senior. First, I want to say Little Norm woulda been here tonight, but he's working on a job over to Nicholasville. Plus, he didn't want to put none a you'uns on the spot with him bein' the cause of this here issue." He stepped forward and slapped the spiral notebook on the table in front of Jerry. "I got a petition here with one hundred eighty-seven names on it what says you'uns ought to give the job to someone from Goose Creek. Ain't no sense in giving Creeker money to outsiders when it ought to stay right here in the Creek." He paused to glance over his shoulder, and seemed encouraged to see several heads nodding in agreement. "What's more, this here RFB business is a bunch of hooey and a waste of taxpayer money. Little Norm's born and raised right here, and he'd get that job done quick-like. Ain't no reason to go involving outsiders."

A few people voiced agreement. Surprised, Al noted Chuck Geddes nodding vigorously. Chuck always seemed like a reasonable man. Surely he wasn't in support of inviting Little Norm to inflict his lack of skill on the town a second time.

Jerry picked up the notebook and flipped

through a few pages. "Thank you, Norman. We will file this petition with the meeting minutes."

"File it and what else?" Norman drew himself up, shoulders stiff. "Can't ignore a hundred and eighty-seven folks."

Gary spoke up. "That's not a majority of the town's population. It's not even ten percent."

Norman turned his glare toward that end of the table. "It's *voters*. You got to do what they say."

"I've got to do what my *conscience* says."

"How many votes put you in that chair, Vandergrift? I'll wager you get a hundred and eighty-seven less come November."

A flush rose on Gary's face. His mouth opened with what was sure to be a heated retort, but Jerry spoke first.

"We don't intend to ignore a single voice," he said smoothly. "I'm sure I speak for all of us when I assure you we will take this petition into account when we cast our votes." He turned his attention pointedly away from Norman to scan the crowd. "Who else would like to speak?"

Woody's hand shot skyward, and Jerry nodded at him.

"My name's Woodson Edwards. My signature's on that petition, and I want to explain why." He half-turned so he addressed the crowd as well as the Council. "I don't necessarily think the town should hire Little Norm to paint the tower." From where he stood, Al saw the shrug of apology Woody directed toward a bristling Norman. "But I do think any job the city hires out ought to go to somebody from Goose Creek, if there's one available. Or at least their kinfolk. We ought to have loyalty toward our town."

Though there was something to be said for loyalty, the "kinfolk" comment pricked Al's memory. Woody had a brother-in-law in the handyman business. He'd been quick to bring him up a few weeks ago when it looked like Al might need someone to do work on the Updyke house. Which, he devoutly hoped, he would not.

When recognized, Pete Lawson glanced at Woody before speaking. "Loyalty's important, I'll grant you that. But when it comes to spending the town's money, I think it's more important to avoid the appearance of favoritism. And we have to consider workmanship too. I don't see anything wrong with accepting bids. If Little Norm comes in with a good bid, he should have the same chance as the others."

Al found himself nodding. Of course, the

only way the Council should consider letting Little Norm touch that water tower was if he volunteered to do it for free. Even then they ought to insist on approving the paint first.

Jerry pointed in Al's direction, and for a startled moment he thought he was being called upon to speak. Then Lucy stepped to the front of the room.

Leonard's lips pursed into a tight bow. "We agreed to keep quiet," he whispered to Al, who didn't hesitate to move forward and take her place.

"Lucy Cardwell," she told Sally, and then faced the crowd. "I think the Council is right. As a business owner in this town, I would hate to be told who to hire. I mean, you all know we hire local help when we can, but look what happened with Fern."

A mumble stirred through the crowd. Fern Wainright, a local teenager, had worked as a cashier at the pharmacy last year until she'd been caught stealing sinus medicine. The police investigation uncovered a meth lab operated by some unsavory fellows in the county outside of town whose main supplier of over-the-counter ingredients was none other than Fern. She was halfway through her sentence in a juvenile detention center in Lexington.

Leonard's eyes squeezed shut. "I can't believe she mentioned Fern," he said in a low voice.

"Now we have Janice, who is trustworthy and reliable," Lucy said. "Is it her fault she's from Frankfort?"

"That's differ'nt." Norman spoke harshly. "You tried hirin' local. Put a sign in the winder an' all. Weren't nobody local wanted the job."

Jerry leveled a stern glance on him. "You've had the floor, Norman. Don't speak out of turn."

"And besides." Lucy appeared to warm to her topic. "Hiring outsiders might end up bringing new residents to Goose Creek. I mean, look at the new veterinarian. She's going to move here."

A grumble sounded among the crowd, louder than any before. Surprised, Al spied more than a few scowls in his immediate vicinity. Millie had mentioned the problems the young woman was having gaining the trust of the Goose Creek pet owners, but he had only listened with half an ear. Judging by the frowns and hissing whispers, the new vet had managed to stomp on quite a few local toes, and not all of them were feline.

Lucy waved a hand. "Whatever you may think of her, at least she is going to bring money into Goose Creek. If this town is going to survive, we need new blood, and new money."

She hurried back toward them and slid between Al and her husband, head ducked. Al gave her a supportive nod. She'd outlined some good points that business owners should consider before shooting off their mouths.

If disaster struck, one day soon he might fall into that category himself. If, on the outside chance, their purchase of the Updyke house went through and Millie's plans for her bed and breakfast came to fruition, he would be a business owner. He didn't plan to hire staff — Lord knew they couldn't afford that — but he'd certainly have to hire people to do the renovation work. Would his friends and neighbors fault him if he looked outside of Goose Creek for help? There really wasn't anyone competent in town. Of course there was Woody's brother-in-law.

Jacob Pulliam took the floor next. "I was undecided when I came here tonight. I see both sides. But while I was listening to everybody talk, something occurred to me. If we make it a rule or a law or something that preference has to be given to Goose Creek residents when it comes to doing work for the town, we're setting a precedent. What'll it be next? Will we make a law that you can't hire any but local boys to mow your grass? If I decide to start me a business doing . . ." He shook his head. "I don't know, maybe digging fence posts. Would you be required to hire me to put in your fence?"

"Ain't no way," shouted someone from the back. "You're too lazy."

Everyone laughed, even Jacob. "You're right about that, but you see what I mean. Think about the complaint about Paul's concrete sidewalk. Making a rule like this will give everybody in town one more reason to complain about their neighbors. The more I think about it, the more I believe nobody ought to tell me how to spend my money."

A half-dozen replies to that argument occurred to Al. Nobody had mentioned mandating private citizens' spending habits, only those involving government funds. Still, it was a logical progression, given the unreasonableness of some of his fellow Creekers. He held his tongue.

The meeting continued far longer than Al's interest in the subject. Almost twenty residents insisted on speaking their piece, even though most of them were only parroting the arguments voiced before them.

Al's feet started to ache, and he was not the only one who shuffled his weight shoe-to-shoe as evening gave way to night. All his favorite Thursday night television shows would be long over and Millie comfortably in bed before he got home.

Finally, when no one else raised their hand, the mayor once again took the floor. "Folks, this has been a terrific discussion. Thanks to all who participated. Does anyone on the Council have any questions?" He glanced left and right. "Okay, then it's time for a motion."

Gary spoke up, his tone saturated with determination. "I move that we approve the RFB and proceed with publishing it."

The audience rumbled. Al glanced at Norman's stormy glare. He'd hate to be sitting in Gary's chair right about now.

"Anyone care to second that motion?" asked Jerry.

Lynn rubbed a hand across her mouth, whirling thoughts apparent on her face. Then, "I second."

Another rumble from the crowd.

With an apprehensive glance toward Norman, Jerry asked, "Further discussion on this issue?"

The silence in the room weighed a ton.

"All right, then." The mayor's spine stiffened, and he set his shoulders. "The motion is to approve the RFB as written and move forward with putting the job of painting of the water tower out to bid. All who approve please signify by raising your hand."

Gary's arm swung straight up, the first in the air. Lynn's followed more slowly, and then Diane's and Phyllis's. All heads turned toward Aaron, who slid down in his chair. His face flaming, he raised his hand slowly.

Last of all, Jerry raised his hand. "Let the minutes show that the vote is unanimous. Now, for the next item —"

"Bull flookies!" Norman's outburst roared in the room. "This still ain't over, Selbo. You mark my words, you ain't heard the last of me."

The man whirled, fury apparent on his face, and pushed his way through the crowd toward the exit.

In the awkward moment after he left the building, Al exchanged a wide-eyed glance with Leonard while between them Lucy had already fished her cell phone out of her purse and was busy tapping with her thumbs. No doubt spreading the juicy news to those not fortunate enough to have witnessed Norman's outburst in person.

CHAPTER ELEVEN

At least there's one good thing about slow days. I certainly get a lot of knitting done. Seated at the reception counter, Millie glanced at the empty chairs in the waiting rooms and snipped the yarn after the final stitch.

She smoothed the miniature cardigan out on the reception counter, admiring the even stitches along the trim. Little Abby was still young enough to be thrilled to receive a handmade sweater from Grandma. At this rate, she'd be able to crank out the matching doll sweater by the time she left work. She whipped out her cell phone and snapped a picture to send to her daughter-in-law up in Cincinnati.

The clinic door swung open and Lucy Cardwell exited, her dachshund draped long-ways along her arm. Susan followed, her typically severe features arranged into a pleasant expression.

"Just cut out the table scraps," she was saying. "Toby's in good health, but his breed is prone to obesity. Now that the weather's turning, a long walk every night will do him wonders."

"Won't hurt Leonard any either." Lucy smiled brightly at Millie. "His spine is fine. I've just got to teach him to stay out from under people's feet." She pulled out her checkbook. "Now, how much do I owe you?"

Susan handed the chart to Millie, who tapped the procedure code into the computer and read the total to Lucy.

"Goodness, is that all?" She smiled at Susan as she scribbled out the check one-handed. "You spent a long time with us and did such a thorough examination."

"He didn't require any X-rays or medications, thank goodness." Susan ran a gentle hand over Toby's head, and then reached into the cookie jar to feed the dog a treat. Toby gulped it down without chewing, which resulted in one of the veterinarian's rare smiles. "Bring him back in a few months, when he's due for his shots."

"I definitely will."

Lucy handed the check to Millie along with a conspiratorial smile. A few phone calls to Millie's friends had brought in a trickle of clients. Bless Lucy for fabricating the story about Toby scrambling under someone's feet and being kicked. Millie had no doubt she would spread the word of Dr. Susan's competence and her caring manner.

With a final wave, Lucy exited and Millie unlocked the cash drawer. "That seemed to go well."

"It did." Susan cocked her head with a puzzled expression. "That's the second 'emergency' visit today, and both turned out to be nothing."

"Don't look a gift horse in the mouth," Millie quoted in a Violet-worthy saying as she placed the check in the drawer.

The front door opened a crack. A small head appeared, and a wide-eyed gaze circled the room. It skittered over Millie and rested on Susan.

"Hello," Susan said in an encouraging tone. "Can we help you with something?"

The child looked vaguely familiar. One of the Wainright brood, perhaps? There were so many she couldn't keep them straight, all except Fern who had made the family name infamous. This one certainly had their look, with her tousled brown hair and heart-shaped face.

The girl regarded Susan silently for a long

moment before slipping her body through the crack. A slight little thing, with stick-like legs and boney arms extending from a short-sleeved dress that was entirely inadequate for this chilly spring day. Her hair could stand a good brushing, and judging by the dirt showing in the cracks of her knees, she would benefit from a long soak in a bathtub. Something in her unkempt appearance softened Millie's heart. She glanced through the window, looking for a car. Surely this child hadn't come alone? Why, she barely looked old enough to go to school.

In her hands she carried a blue plastic box with a vented top. "Otis is sick."

Susan regarded the child seriously. "Well, that's not good. Would you like me to take a look at him?" The wide-set eyes narrowed, and she continued. "I'm Dr. Susan, the new veterinarian."

Giving a tentative nod, the girl shifted the box to one arm and removed the lid with the other. Susan stepped forward to look inside. Millie craned her neck, but couldn't see what manner of pet Otis was.

"Hmm. I'll need to conduct a thorough examination." She straightened. "Millie, will you please create a new patient file for Otis and . . ." She looked back at the girl.

"What's your name?"

"Willow Wainright." The girl's reply confirmed Millie's suspicions. Worried creases appeared above finely-shaped eyebrows. "How much will it cost?"

Susan folded an arm across her middle and propped her other elbow on it, tapping at her lips thoughtfully with a forefinger. "Have you been here before, Willow?" The child shook her head. "Then you're in luck. Normally the exam is thirty-five dollars, but because I'm new to town we're running an introductory special. The first exam for a new patient is free."

And without even consulting Daddy. Good for you.

Willow's eyes widened, and relief cleared her brow.

"Of course, if any medication is required, you'll have to pay for that. But we can negotiate terms, if necessary."

Millie held back a smile at the girl's serious expression as she nodded and followed Susan toward the exam rooms. Her estimation of her new boss rose considerably. Susan's manner toward Willow was perfect, completely professional and without a hint of condescension. When she told everyone about this, the vet would gain brownie points for sure.

Susan opened the clinic door and directed Willow to take Otis to exam room one, then spoke to Millie in a low voice.

"Quick. Do a quick Google search for anything you can find about caring for hermit crabs."

"You bet. Is this your first crab?"

Susan nodded.

"Well, I'm sure it won't be your last crabby patient." Chuckling at her own joke, Millie pulled the keyboard toward her while Susan followed Willow. She found a website called Basic Crab Care and printed off several pages, which she delivered to exam room one. When she returned to the counter, the phone began to ring.

"Goose Creek Animal Clinic."

"Millie?"

Hear heart leapt when she recognized the voice. "Louise! Tell me you have good news."

"I do, actually. I've had a request to show your house this evening at six o'clock."

Millie glanced at the wall clock. Ten after three. That gave her just under three hours to get ready.

"That's great," she told the realtor. "I'll be ready."

"You know you can't be there, right? And turn on all the lights, and —"

"I've done my research," she assured Louise. "I know how to make the house bright and cheery and welcoming. How long should we plan to stay away?"

"Oh, half an hour or so. Of course if you come home and see a car in the driveway, just keep driving."

"Of course."

Which scent should she burn? Cinnamon Cider, maybe? No, cinnamon gave some people a headache. Something peaceful and homey, like Sugar Cookie. It contained a hint of vanilla, which was universally appealing. Definitely Sugar Cookie.

Louise was still talking. "— not discouraged. After all, the Forsythe property is really a fluke. Things like that don't happen very often."

Millie straightened to attention. "Things like what? What happened to the Forsythe property?"

A pause. "I assumed you'd know, since you work for Dr. Forsythe."

"I haven't talked to him since he went on vacation. What about their house?"

"It's sold. Their agent told me this morning. They received an offer yesterday and accepted it last night."

A sense of injustice welled up inside Millie. Her fingers clutched the edge of the desk, nails folding against the hard surface. Her house had been on the market for ten whole days, and tonight was the first time anyone had even requested to see it. Doc and Lizzie listed theirs three days ago on their way out of town and they'd already accepted an offer?

"Don't be upset, Millie." Louise's voice took on a soothing tone. "Theirs was an unusual situation. The buyer is someone they knew from one of Dr. Forsythe's professional organizations. He apparently sent out an e-mail to his contact list, and it paid off."

An e-mail. Why hadn't she thought of that? Not that she knew many people outside of Goose Creek, and all of those already knew her house was up for sale. She didn't belong to professional organizations like Doc.

She forced an even tone. "I'm happy for them. We'll keep our fingers crossed for tonight's showing."

"That's right. I'll let you know how it goes."

"Talk to you later." Millie pressed the button to disconnect the call, and then released it to dial Albert's office number. The call rang and rang, her irritation mounting. Just when she expected to hear her husband's voicemail recording, an entirely different voice answered.

"Heeeeeeelllllo, Richardson's desk. Franklin Thacker speaking."

The tone was upbeat and cheerful, the words delivered in a sing-song tone that brought an answering smile to her face. The man's name sounded familiar, but she didn't think they'd ever met.

"This is Millie Richardson. Albert's wife."

"Mrs. R!" Franklin's exclamation was one of utter delight. "I'd started to think Bert was making you up."

"Bert?"

"An inside joke." His hee-haw ended in a snort. "Your hubby's away from his office. Headed to the men's room a few minutes ago. I expect he'll be a while, since he was carrying a copy of the *Wall Street Journal.*" Another chuckle and snort. "What can I do for you?"

"Could you pass along a message, please?" While she talked, she fished her appointment calendar out of her purse and clicked open a pen. She intended to keep a record of the showings. "Tell him someone's coming to look at the house tonight at six o'clock, so he can't come home."

"All righty, then. Writing now. *Bert, the Mrs. says do not come home tonight.*" This

171

time the laughter could only be described as a guffaw. "Just kidding, Mrs. R. I'll give him the scoop. Showing your house, huh? That mean you're selling it?"

"Albert hasn't mentioned it?" Irritated, she clenched her fists. She didn't have many contacts outside of their community, but Albert did. The least he could do was let people know. "Yes, our house has been on the market for over a week. We hope to buy a lovely old Victorian-era home here in Goose Creek." No need to mention the B&B plans.

"Goose Creek, huh? Nice little town. The missus and I come to the Fall Festival every year."

"It's our big event," she said. "Well, if you know of anyone looking for a beautiful three bedroom two bathroom house, be sure to let them know."

"I'll do it," he promised. "What time is Bert allowed to come home?"

Bert. Albert must think a lot of Franklin to allow him the use of a nickname. Odd that he never mentioned the man.

"I don't really know." Millie tapped the pen on the desk. "On second thought, tell him to come at the regular time, but meet me at the Whistlestop. I'll treat him to dinner out." That would put him in a good mood, since the chicken and dumplings at the Whistlestop Diner were his favorite.

"Whistlestop it is." He chuckled again. The man certainly laughed a lot. Actually, that annoying snort would probably get on her nerves after a while, which was unkind of her.

"Thank you, Franklin. I hope we can meet sometime."

"That would be my pleasure, Mrs. R."

She'd just hung up the phone when Susan and Willow returned to the reception area.

"Come back tomorrow and I'll have that saltwater all ready for you. I'm sure that will perk Otis right up."

Willow clutched the plastic box to her chest. "I didn't know he needed saltwater. It's a good thing I came, huh?"

"It is, indeed. I'll see you tomorrow." She let the child out, and then collapsed against the door. "Whew. Thanks for the quick research. I hated to tell that little girl I'd never treated a hermit crab. I just hope the saltwater does the trick."

"Saltwater?"

Susan nodded. "Once I looked at the pages you printed, I remembered reading about it in one of my earlier classes. You're supposed to keep a sponge saturated with saltwater and the temp in the low seventies.

That gives the crabitat a tropical-like atmosphere."

Millie's lips twitched. "The crabitat, huh? Sounds like a good name for Albert when he gets in one of his complaining moods." She straightened. "I hate to ask, but would it be all right if I leave a little early? We've got someone coming to look at the house tonight, and I want to tidy up a bit."

"Of course." Susan waved a hand toward the empty waiting rooms. "I think I can handle the crowd."

"At least we've had fewer cancellations today. And even some new appointments."

"That's true." She heaved herself away from the door and headed for the back. When she reached the corner of the reception desk, she paused, her gaze averted. "I know you've been making calls on my behalf. Thank you."

Millie smiled at the girl. She looked so young and . . . well, helpless. "I'm glad to help."

With a nod, the veterinarian continued toward her office. "If you need anything from Lexington, let me know. After I close up I'm running over to the pet supply store to pick up saltwater solution and a sea sponge."

And no charge to Willow, probably. How

sweet. If the town knew of Susan's soft heart, they'd welcome her with open arms.

Well, that was something Millie could do — make sure they knew.

"Really, Millie? Franklin Thacker?"

Al fixed a pained expression on his wife. The restaurant booth's light dangled between them, casting a yellowish glow on her face and turning her eyes into dark orbs. Just then her eyebrows were arched innocently above them.

"He seemed friendly enough. And he called you Bert."

He winced. "He does it to plague me. Did he laugh a lot?"

Her lips twitched sideways. "And snorted."

With a shudder, Al unrolled his silverware. "He spent the afternoon drilling me about our plans."

Now her mouth tightened irritably. "Why haven't you told anyone at work about the house being for sale?"

"Because it's none of their business. I prefer to keep my personal and professional lives separate. Especially when it comes to Thacker." He smoothed the napkin in his lap and changed the subject. "How long do we have to stay gone?"

"A long time, hopefully. That means they like the house." She laid out her cutlery, knife and spoon on one side, fork on the other, and then reached across the table to arrange his as well. "Violet is going to text me when they leave."

A glance at his watch told him the time: five fifty-seven. In three minutes his home would be invaded. Strangers tromping through their bedrooms, inspecting their bathrooms, peeking in their closets. The whole business left him distinctly uncomfortable.

Millie, too, glanced at her watch. "I hope they like Sugar Cookie."

He cast a startled glance across the booth. "You baked them cookies?" She never baked *him* cookies anymore.

"No, silly. I burned Sugar Cookie scent in my warmer. A pleasant aroma is supposed to welcome people when they step inside. That, and a bright, warm light. I turned all the lights on, and even put some soothing music on the stereo."

All the lights burning. That dial on the electric meter was probably whirling like a windmill. He held his tongue, but didn't suppress an aggrieved sigh.

The server arrived with their iced tea and set a slab of warm corn-bread between them. Al ignored Millie's disapproving frown and ordered a side of mashed potatoes and gravy with his chicken and dumplings. His private property was, at that very moment, being put on public display. He deserved all the starch he wanted. In a minor attempt to erase the crevasses between her eyes, he requested a light vinaigrette for his salad in place of his usual bleu cheese.

The young man left, still writing on his pad, and a woman stepped into his place. Hazel Duncan, who covered reception at the animal clinic on Saturdays. An outspoken liberal, she and Al had butted heads over politics more than once before acknowledging the futility of trying to convince each other. They had maintained a satisfactory arrangement of mutual avoidance for years.

"Millie! Good to see you." Her gaze traveled the distance of her nose toward Al. "Hello."

He nodded more or less pleasantly and made a show of selecting a yellow packet from the sugar container.

"We haven't had a chance to talk in ages." Millie settled back in the high booth and looked up at the woman. "So what do you think of our new boss?"

"Hard to tell." Hazel scrubbed a hand through her spikey brown locks. "She's kind of a mouse."

"Oh, no." Millie rushed to the new vet's defense. "She's a bit hesitant at first, but she has such a good heart."

"You'd know better since you work with her more." The woman shrugged, and her gaze slid again toward Al. "So what side have you two come down on?"

Millie and Al exchanged a blank look.

"Side?"

"You know. This water tower thing." She waved vaguely in the general direction of the unseen tower. "I admit at first I was hesitant to align with Pilkington be-cause . . ." Her eyes rolled toward the beamed ceiling. "It's Norman, after all. But once I put my noggin to noodling the issue, I agree with him."

Her words surprised Al out of his deter-mined silence. "You do?" If he'd been asked, he would have pegged Hazel for the give-everybody-a-shot-at-the-job woman.

"Not that I think we ought to hire Little Norm, you understand." A shudder shook her wide shoulders. "Lord only knows what we'd end up with next time. But I'm all about governmental oversight." She leaned over and planted her hands on the table. "I

178

mean look what we've got here. A bunch of local yokels sitting around a folding table twice a month and deciding how to spend our tax dollars. We don't even know if they're Democrats or Republicans, just average Joes and Josettes who change diapers during the day and pretend to be politicians at night."

A direct slap at Diane Hudson, whose third child had just started to toddle.

"I'm sure they do the best they can," put in his kind-hearted wife.

" 'Course they do, but they're untrained. They need rules in place to keep them honest, that's all I'm saying. They ought to have procedures to follow before they start writing checks."

Al couldn't hold his tongue. "That's not what Norman is proposing. He believes the city should be forced to hire residents over outsiders."

Hazel rounded on him, eyes flashing. "So you're against the proposed legislation?"

"I didn't say that." He splayed his hands in her direction to ward off the accusation. "I'm staying completely neutral. But what you're describing isn't what I understood Norman's position to be."

She planted a sturdy hand on her hip. "Look, we all know what Norman wants.

He wants his kid to make a buck off of Goose Creek." She shrugged. "If I had a kid, I'd probably want the same thing. But this issue is bigger than the water tower. It's the beginning of change, a step in the right direction. First we get them to agree to follow a set of established rules before they make decisions involving our money. *Then* we work on fine-tuning those rules 'til we get 'em where they should be."

Twisted logic, but in a way it made sense. Of course, the Council already had procedures, but since he had no idea what they were he couldn't comment on them one way or the other.

The server returned and edged Hazel out of the way to place their salads in front of them.

She continued talking, apparently determined to deliver her opinion whether they wanted to hear it or not. "Which side of the street are you two going to march on? If you take my advice, you'll choose a side and skedaddle over to it quick. 'Cause you know what happens if you stand around in the middle of the street in Goose Creek." Her gaze ping-ponged between Al and Millie. "You get run over by a train."

With that parting shot, which Al had to admit was clever, she drifted away. As the server set a miniature pitcher of salad dressing in front of him, a double-ding erupted from Millie's phone. She snatched it up and punched at the screen.

Crestfallen, she looked up at him. "They just left. They didn't even stay fifteen minutes."

Relief loosened the muscles in Al's neck. A bullet dodged, thank goodness.

But he found it hard to enjoy his chicken and dumplings with Millie looking so crestfallen.

CREATING A HEALTHY CRABITAT

Creating a comfy, healthy home for your hermit crab will ensure that he enjoys a long, happy life. You will need:

Container: Most experts agree that the plastic container your crab came home in is inadequate for his long-term health and happiness. Instead, get him a glass aquarium with a lid.

Substrate: Hermit crabs like to burrow and crawl. Cover the bottom of your crabitat with terrarium sand, or with a substrate made specifically for hermit crabs.

Water bowl: Make it shallow enough that he can climb in and out of it easily, and won't drown. Keep the dish filled with bottled or distilled water, which is chlorine-free.

Sponge: Place a natural sponge in a dish to slow the dehydration process, and keep it saturated with salt water.

Salt Water: Crabs require both fresh and salt water. You can purchase a salt solution from your local pet store. *Do not* use table salt, which will make your crab sick, or even kill him.

Toys: Crabs need to roam and climb. Give him rough barks, climbing toys, shelters, and sanitized branches.

Temperature: The ideal temperature is no lower than 75 degrees. Place your crabitat in a warm corner in your house. Or you can purchase an under-tank heater or a reptile light to regulate the temperature. Do invest in a thermometer so you can make sure your crab isn't too hot or too cold.

Humidity: Your crab thrives in a sub-tropic environment where the relative humidity is around 70%. To accomplish this, you can purchase a bubble bowl, or simply make it a habit to mist your crabitat daily with warm water.

Extra Shells: As crabs grow, they leave their old shells and relocate to new ones. Include a few shells in a variety of sizes larger than your crab's current one so he has a bit of choice.

Space: Crabs also need room to roam in

order to burn energy. Make sure your crabitat includes some empty space in case your crab wants to indulge in the occasional sprint.

Food: For the best results, purchase crab food from your local pet supply store. This will provide all the nutrients your crab needs. Then supplement with natural fruits and vegetables such as berries, bananas, cucumbers, and spinach or kale leaves.

Companions: Hermit crabs love company! Since you've set up an appropriate crabitat, get a few friends for your crab.

CHAPTER TWELVE

All through the morning, Al puttered around the empty house and struggled to ignore a nagging sense of foreboding. Millie had left him to his own devices and gone off to meet the inspector at the Updyke property. She had not bothered to hide her irritation at his refusal to go along.

"I'm not spending my Saturday watching somebody crawl through insulation and turn on water faucets," he'd told her. "Saturdays are my only chance to sleep in."

The clatter of pots and pans from the kitchen rendered sleep an impossibility, so he'd arisen at his usual six-thirty. The noise was definitely an expression of his wife's displeasure, since breakfast turned out to be cold cereal and a piece of toast. Nothing requiring pots *or* pans. Millie's lips had formed a reproving line which she swiped at his cheek in a perfunctory goodbye kiss. At least she'd taken her dog along.

He had just unearthed the box of bird feeders from the shelves that lined the garage when the electric whirr of the opener erupted to life. Sunlight flooded the space, and he watched as the front tire of her pepto-pink Volkswagen rolled to a stop against the two-by-four he kept in place so she wouldn't smash into his workbench. The happy smile she flashed through the windshield tightened a knot in his stomach. Apparently the inspection had gone well.

"Good news," she announced as she exited the car. "The electricity and plumbing are in excellent shape. Apparently Mr. Updyke updated both shortly before he died."

Al tried to keep his shoulders from drooping. He'd counted on the huge cost of replacing ancient wiring to further his cause. Or at least rusty plumbing.

"Lead paint?" he asked hopefully.

With a bright smile, Millie shook her head and opened the back door to let Rufus out. "The wallpaper is ancient, of course, but the house was repainted in the late seventies. No trace of lead." She waved a folder in his direction. "I have the inspector's report here. Let's have a cup of coffee while we go over it."

The black cloud of doom crept over him

as he followed her into the kitchen. She set the folder on the table in front of his chair and headed for the coffeemaker. Al lowered himself onto the cushion. A thread of hope dangled before him when he flipped open the front cover and located the inspector's list of items. It was three full pages long. Surely there would be *something* expensive in there, some showstopper. As he scanned the list, the thread unraveled.

"The roof has to be replaced," he commented.

"We knew that." She plugged in the coffeemaker and pressed the switch. "But that's the biggest thing."

"The furnace is seventeen years old."

"True, but it's a high-end one, and in good shape. The man said it should last another ten years at least, and probably longer."

"Hmm." He studied page after page, zeroing in on the checkmarks in the 'Unsatisfactory' column. There were plenty. Chandeliers with wiring issues, loose banisters and railings, cracked outlet casings. The garbage disposal needed replacing and one of the burners on the stove didn't work. But besides the roof, no single deficiency would have a price tag big enough to justify his refusal to move ahead with the deal.

"That roof —" he began, but Millie cut him off.

"I've already contacted that handyman I told you about. Hinkle the Handyman. He's coming Monday to give us an estimate. On everything, in fact." She set a steaming mug on the table and slid the fake sugar bowl toward him. "He's never worked with those decorative slate shingles, so he'll give us a good price since the job will give him experience."

He caught her gaze in a stern one of his own. "I'm not interested in restoring the roof to its original condition. Just putting on one that will keep the rain off our heads."

An argument appeared on her features. She opened her mouth, but closed it a second later. Her head dipped forward in acknowledgement. Somewhat mollified, Al continued his perusal of the inspection document. He'd expected more of a fuss.

"I don't know, Millie." He closed the folder and took his time stirring sweetener into his coffee. "The cost of repairing all those things will add up quickly."

"We don't have to do everything at once, just a bedroom and the kitchen. Enough that we can live there comfortably for a while. We have years to get the rest done."

Cocking his head, he gave her a cynical

look. Did she really think he'd go for that? Once she started a project, she would hound him to the ends of the earth until it was finished. But since she returned his stare with wide eyes and covered his hand with her warm one, his reply went unspoken.

Heaving a sigh, he pushed the inspection report away. "Let's see what your handyman says on Monday."

His reward was the appearance of those kissable dimples that never failed to soften him.

They flashed out of existence. "Oh, I almost forgot. Louise called. We have another showing today at three-thirty."

A scowl weighed heavy on his face. "I want to put up the feeders this afternoon."

"Can't it wait? Please?"

Another dramatic sigh. Goodness, he was starting to puff like a steam engine. "I suppose."

"Good. Violet and I are going to run over to Lexington to look at wallpaper. Would you like to join us?"

"Not a chance. I drive that road ten times a week as it is. I have no desire to do it on the weekend."

"Then you'll need to find something to do for an hour or so. And take Rufus."

At the mention of his name, the dog raised its head from yet another nap and turned a liquid brown gaze toward them. Deepening his scowl, Al sipped from his mug. More strangers tromping through his house, disrupting his Saturday while he was left baby-sitting the world's smelliest mutt. The gloomy cloud that darkened his mood grew heavier, and he couldn't shake the feeling that he was being shoved closer and closer to the doom that would render him the poverty-stricken owner of an ancient real estate monstrosity.

Al left Rufus soaking up the sunshine outside Cardwell's and entered the store a few minutes after four. He'd taken a detour to walk by the Updyke house on the off chance that he'd discover the roof had collapsed in the hours since the inspector left. No such luck.

Mid-afternoon at the soda fountain wasn't a peak time, so the place was practically deserted. An out-of-towner, a woman dressed in jeans and boots, sat at one of the tables sipping coffee and glancing around with a half-smile on her face. The old-fashioned charm often hit visitors like that, though Creekers had gotten used to it. He slid onto an empty stool between Woody and Miles, who had perched on opposite ends of the counter.

"Got any pie?" he asked Lucy.

"You know it."

She produced one from the icebox and sliced a generous wedge. Thick cherry juice oozed from beneath the browned top crust, and his mouth flooded at the sight.

"Heated, please, with ice cream."

She gave him a look from over the top of her glasses. "Millie will skin me alive if you spoil your supper."

"I can handle it," he assured her.

Moments later she set a dish on the paper placemat in front of him, a generous scoop of vanilla already melting on the steamy dessert. "It's sugar free," she announced.

Enthusiasm dampened slightly, he regarded the dish. "The pie or ice cream?"

"Both. And it's frozen yogurt."

There were disadvantages to living in a small town, chief among them the fact that his wife had agents everywhere. He took a cautious bite, and his trepidation dimmed. Delicious. He could almost forget it was sugar free.

Woody twisted sideways on his stool. "So what side are you camping on, Al?"

Though he knew immediately what the

man meant, he played dumb. "Side of what?"

A grunt sounded from the opposite end of the counter. "You know," said Miles. "Are you with the Council or the rabble-rousers like Norman and Woody?"

The temperature in the room warmed in the fiery glare the two men exchanged.

"I'm neutral," Al put in quickly, and sliced off a second bite.

"That's a cop-out." Woody snatched a half-empty glass off the counter. "You're gonna have to take a side sooner or later."

He made a show of chewing before he answered. "I don't see why."

" 'Cause you do, that's all," Miles insisted. "You can't stand around and let everybody else fight this war for you."

War. The word hung ominously in the air. This water tower thing was getting out of hand. It was starting to feel like the conflict over Main Street's traffic flow. Would Mayor Selbo end up like his predecessor, forced to sell his house and leave Goose Creek? Al hoped not. Jerry was a nice guy. With an effort, Al ignored the accusation and held his silence.

Bells jingled as he took another bite.

"Would you look at this place," exclaimed a woman's voice. "It's an old-fashioned soda fountain. I wonder if they have chocolate malts."

"We sure do." Lucy aimed a smile behind his head. "Best you've ever tasted."

"Give us two," announced a man as the door slammed shut.

Al's jaw froze mid-chew. He knew that voice.

"Well, would you lookie here! It's the man himself. Sugar, this is my buddy Bert." A heavy hand pounded Al's back. "Just came from your place, old man. Nice digs."

No. It can't be.

Woody, Miles, and Lucy all turned toward him with various expressions of surprised amusement. Al snatched up his water glass and gulped the half-chewed pie down before it choked him. Fear slowed his movements as he twisted on the stool. Before him stood none other than Franklin Thacker. Here. In Cardwell's. On a Saturday.

"Oh, very nice." The woman gushed and smiled wide enough to reveal lipstick marks on a set of buck teeth. "We just *love* it."

"You were in . . ." His throat closed around the words, and he took another swig of water. ". . . my house?"

"Did we stutter?" Franklin pounded his back a second time. "Or is your hearing going?"

The woman giggled and planted an elbow in Franklin's ribs. "Don't insult him, sweetie pie. After all, we might end up being neighbors."

Ringing in Al's ears drowned out the sound of his pounding pulse. Franklin Thacker, the most obnoxious man in the world, his neighbor?

"Now, Sugar Bear, don't be giving anything away before we even make an offer. We don't want to tip our hand." A loud guffaw, punctuated by snorts, filled the previously peaceful sanctuary of Cardwell Drug Store.

The pie soured in Al's stomach.

"I won't accept it." Al shoved the document away with more force than necessary. Papers fluttered across the kitchen table.

Louise's professional mask evaporated. She gaped. "But it's a full-price offer. Do you know how rare that is?"

Seated to his right, Millie sat ramrod straight in her chair, arms folded. Fire flashed in the stare she fixed on him.

"I don't care," Al told the realtor. "This is *Franklin Thacker* we're talking about. You don't understand." He grasped about for an argument that would communicate the depth of his feelings on the matter. "He calls me Bert," he ended lamely.

"He's friendly." Millie snapped through gritted teeth.

"It's a show." Al turned to her with an imploring gaze. "He ingratiates himself at first so he can plague you with his obnoxious personality later."

Louise snatched the pen out of her blonde bun and clicked it repeatedly while she regained an expression of cool professionalism. "You don't have to live with him. You won't even be living in the same neighborhood."

"That's right." He turned on Millie. "Do you want to inflict Thacker on Violet, your best friend?"

She drew a breath through flaring nostrils and did not reply.

"Besides," continued the realtor, "you'll be making a very nice profit on your house at his expense. Won't that be satisfying?"

Ah, a direct blow aimed at his vulnerable spot — his bank account. "The idea of him living here, in *my* house, grilling burgers on *my* deck, trimming *my* bushes . . ." He gave an expansive shudder. "No amount of money is worth that."

"You promised." Millie punched his forearm repeatedly with her finger. "You laid out a ridiculous set of conditions, and every one has been met. You never expected that, so now you've come up with a final lame attempt to renege on your promise. You gave your *word,* Albert."

Al rubbed the stinging place where her fingernail had poked his skin. An unfair accusation. His motives — to maintain marital peace and harmony — were pure. He opened his mouth to say so.

Then he closed it again. Were his motives truly unselfish? He'd specified conditions he never thought would be met. His aim had been to appease his wife, true, but without any real intention to sacrifice his own plans. An uncomfortable feeling set him fidgeting in his chair. He'd manipulated a solution that would put him in a favorable light in Millie's eyes, but without expecting to go through with his end of the bargain.

"There's something else you may want to consider." Louise broke into his uncomfortable thoughts. "My contract with you outlines specific conditions for the sale of this house. I've delivered an offer that meets those conditions. If you reject it, you're obligated to compensate me at the rate we agreed on." She gave an apologetic shrug. "Business is business."

His gaze volleyed between the two of them. From the beginning they'd joined sides against him.

And, he realized as his heart sank to the vicinity of his shoes, *they've won.*

A promise was a promise, after all. Especially a promise to his wife.

Utterly defeated, he bowed his head. "Where do I sign?"

CHAPTER THIRTEEN

Monday morning arrived with a sky full of sunshine and a future bright with promise. Millie hummed a hymn from yesterday's service as she stowed her purse in the file cabinet and turned toward the computer, a bulging baggie of cookies in her hand.

Susan emerged from the back room and greeted her with her usual solemn, "Good morning." Then she caught sight of the baggie, and her face brightened. "Did you make cookies?"

"Yes, but they're not for us. They're dog cookies."

"Oh."

At the sight of the girl's disappointed expression, Millie vowed to arrive tomorrow with a tray of people treats. "How was your weekend?"

"Okay, I guess." The slender shoulders shrugged. "I found an apartment. It's on Walnut Street, so I can walk to work."

Possible rentals flickered through Millie's thoughts. "Betty and Ralph Hunsaker's place?"

Susan nodded. "It's just a couple of rooms above the garage, but that's all I need. They seem like nice people."

"They are," Millie agreed. "They built that apartment for Betty's mother, but then the poor dear broke a hip and couldn't climb the stairs so she moved to Tennessee to live with her son."

"That's what they said. Daddy liked them."

Millie maintained a pleasant expression. "Your father was in town?"

"Yes, he came up yesterday to help me find a suitable place to live." Her lips twisted. "Not that there was much to see."

"It's a small town," Millie agreed. "What a shame I didn't get to meet him."

She was about to ask what he thought of Goose Creek when the door opened. They both turned, expecting to see a pet owner, but a young man entered with no animal in sight. A pair of worn but clean jeans rode low on his hips, held in place by a leather belt with a Harley Davidson buckle encircling a trim waist. He fixed Millie with a clear blue gaze.

"Mrs. Richardson?" His deep voice held

an engaging touch of gravel.

The handyman from Frankfort. Thirty minutes early. "Mr. Hinkle?"

"Call me Justin, ma'am." He stepped inside, a pair of heavy work boots thudding on the floor, and approached with his hand extended. Millie shook it — hers disappeared in its surprisingly gentle but gigantic depths — and gestured toward Susan.

"This is Dr. Susan Jeffries."

Susan's eyes grew wide enough to overtake her face. Her lips parted slightly and froze. What was wrong with the girl? Millie glanced back at Justin to find him returning the stare, his expression openly admiring.

Goodness. If the sparks between these two get any warmer, I'll have to call the fire department.

He recovered himself. "A pleasure to meet you, Dr. Jeffries."

The hand he extended hung between them for a long moment. Then Susan's mouth closed and she gave herself a visible shake.

"You too." The poor girl winced when her voice squeaked. She took his hand and then sucked in an audible breath. The handshake drew out, neither participant releasing the other's grasp. Hiding a delighted smile,

Millie busied herself with the task of unzipping the baggie and emptying the cookies into the doggie treat jar.

Susan finally withdrew her hand. "Do you have a dog?"

"Excuse me?"

"Your pet, I mean. Is it a dog?"

He looked around the room as if noticing where he was for the first time. Again, Millie hid a smile. Budding attraction was so much fun to watch.

"Oh. No. I mean, I don't have a pet. I'd like to, but it's . . ." He jerked his head. "What I mean is, do I need one?"

At Susan's confused expression, Millie broke into the conversation. "Justin does construction work. He's in town to give me an estimate on repairs to the house my husband and I are buying."

"So you're not here for me." Susan looked completely crestfallen, and then seemed to realize what she'd said. She stiffened with a jerk. "I mean, you're not here for a veterinary visit."

A disarming smile crept over Justin's features. "If I needed a vet, you'd be the first one I called."

Roses erupted in Susan's cheeks, the result charming. Disarmed, the girl retreated a step, obviously ready to make a dash for her office. "I've got some, uh, some paperwork. Back . . . there." She pointed vaguely behind her, her gaze still glued to Justin. "So, I'll just leave . . ." Another step. Then she halted and snapped her fingers, her gaze flying toward Millie. "I forgot to tell you. Doc called on Saturday. They're extending their stay in Florida until the twenty-sixth. Would you mind handling the afternoons a bit longer?"

Full days at work really didn't suit Millie. She missed her afternoons alone in the house before Albert got home from work. Especially now that she had to start packing away a lifetime's worth of accumulated possessions. But she couldn't leave the poor girl high and dry.

She pasted on a smile. "Certainly."

"Thank you." With another shy glance at the handyman, she fled.

Justin straightened and cleared his throat. "I stopped to pick up that list you mentioned on the phone."

"Of course." Millie retrieved the inspection document from her handbag. "My realtor is planning to meet you at the house at ten to let you in."

He glanced at his watch. "That's fine. I'll go on over and see the outside first. It'll probably take me a couple of hours, and then I'll head back to my office to put together some prices. Unless I find something I need to research, I'll have my bid ready by late afternoon."

"That's fine. You have our number."

He nodded, and continued to stand in front of her, his gaze returning to the clinic door through which Susan had disappeared.

"Have you visited Goose Creek before?" Millie asked.

The question seemed to remind him of her presence. He looked at her with a start. "Oh. No, ma'am. This is my first time." Once again, he looked toward the back. "I hope it won't be the last."

She didn't bother to hide her smile this time.

Violet called that afternoon.

"Something's brewing. I was over in Frankfort getting my tags renewed and I saw Eulie at the *Pic Pac*." Her emphasis flooded the words with import.

The meaning became instantly clear to Millie. Creekers either shopped at the Kroger in nearby Versailles or made the longer trek to Lexington. For Norman Pilkington's wife to go all the way to Frankfort definitely looked suspicious.

But there could be a logical reason.

"Maybe she had business in Frankfort too, and stopped to pick up a few things."

"Nope. I spied her car in the parking lot so I went in." A dramatic pause. *"Her shopping cart was full."*

"Oh my." Millie toyed with a paperclip, thoughts whirling. "Still, there's no law that says —"

"I confronted her," Violet announced. "Asked her point-blank why she was shopping there instead of the Kroger store. She turned red as a beet and stuttered like a nail gun."

When on one of her cross-examination binges, Violet could be quite intimidating. Poor, shy Eulie wouldn't stand a chance.

"What did she say?"

"A lame excuse about a tomato sale, which I refused to accept, and finally the truth came out." Drama tinged her voice. "Norman *made* her go to Frankfort."

"Why would he do that?"

"To keep her quiet." Violet lowered her voice to barely above a whisper. "She knows something, and he doesn't want her telling it."

Glancing around the empty waiting room, Millie whispered back, "What does she know?"

"There's something planned for Saturday.

Norman's been holding secret meetings in the barn all weekend."

A delicious chill swept across Millie's skin. "What are they meeting about?"

Violet replied in a normal tone, disappointment heavy in her voice. "I couldn't pry it out of her. Said Norman would skin her alive if she told. But she did say if I have any errands to do out of town, Saturday would be a good day to get them done."

The paperclip was now a straight wire, and she used it to pick absently at the ragged edges of the message pad. Who could she call to find out? "Who do we know in Norman's camp?"

"Would Hazel tell?"

"Possibly." Millie reviewed the conversation with Hazel at the Whistlestop. Did her urging them to take sides have an unspoken purpose? Was she, in fact, feeling them out to see if it was safe to invite them to these top-secret meetings in the Pilkington barn? If she'd been inclined to share details, she would have done so then. "What about Sharon Geddes? Albert said Chuck was in Norman's camp at the Council meeting."

"Good idea. You want to call?"

Susan emerged from the clinic then, frowning over a folder. The girl seemed determined to memorize the contents of every pet file in the cabinet, though Millie couldn't imagine why. Probably bored, the poor dear. "I really can't right now."

"I'll do it." Violet sounded positively gleeful at the prospect. "I'm sure I can get her to spill the beans."

"Let me know the minute you find out anything." Millie hung up and turned her attention to Susan.

"According to the chart, we haven't seen this animal in over two years. I've noticed quite a few like that." She closed the folder and read from the tab. "Tiger McCoy."

"Oh, that's Christine McCoy's beagle. She works at a bank in Lexington, so she started taking him to one of those drop-off pet store clinics nearby. She said we close too early and she can't get back here in time."

"I don't have a problem staying open a bit later." Susan's eyes brightened as an idea occurred. "Do you think there are others who go somewhere else because of scheduling problems?"

"I'm sure of it. Doc and Lizzie were both adamant about locking the doors right at five o'clock."

"Maybe I could give them a call." She seemed almost fearful that Millie would veto the idea. "You know, kind of introduce myself and tell them I'm happy to work around their schedules."

"An excellent idea." Millie poured on the enthusiasm, pleased when Susan's face lit. "If you want, we can go over the files together and I'll tell you what I know about each one before you call."

"I'll start on a list right away." She half-turned, and then stopped as though a thought had just occurred to her. To Millie's sharp eye, the gesture looked a tad put-on. "Uh, you know that guy who was here earlier?"

"Justin?" Millie affected a pleasantly blank expression, though she had a hard time biting back a chuckle. "He seemed like a nice young man. He certainly is nice looking."

"Is he? I didn't notice." At least she had the grace to blush when she lied. "You mentioned some work he'll be doing for you."

"That depends on his prices. But I hope he's affordable. I rather liked him."

In fact, she had decided to hire Justin Hinkle when she first heard about him, no matter what Albert said. They'd argued over the issue last night when he insisted she get estimates from at least two other sources. A complete waste of time, in her opinion.

Susan seemed to be struggling to come up with a reply, so Millie added, "Do you have some work that needs to be done?"

Her face cleared as she leaped on the question. "Yes. Exactly. I noticed that, uh, the knob on the door of my office is loose."

"I noticed that myself," Millie agreed, and then added graciously, "Maybe he could look at that toilet too. I think the water level needs adjusting."

"I've thought the same thing." The enthusiasm in her nod definitely exceeded what would be normal for a toilet repair.

"He said he'd call with his bid this evening," Millie said. "If you want, I could ask his fee for repairs like that."

The tension in her shoulders relaxed, and a smile transformed her rather severe features. "That would be good. Thank you."

Carrying her folder, she left in the direction of her office. Millie's grin broke to the fore. Did young people realize how transparent they were? She pulled the trash can from beneath the desk and swept the mangled paperclip and confetti in.

The door swung open, and she looked up to find Susan's head peeking into the room. Smile gone, the lines had returned to her forehead.

"On second thought, never mind. No sense wasting the money. Daddy can fix those things next time he comes."

The door swung shut.

Daddy again.

With a thud, Millie shoved the trash can back in place. If *Daddy* were here right now, she'd give him an earful.

"She wouldn't budge," Violet announced over the phone that evening. "Lips shut tighter than a clam. Tongue frozen over like a pond in January. Silent as the grave. Quiet as —"

"I get the point." Millie used a firmer tone than normal. Sometimes Violet could get carried away.

Albert tore his gaze away from the television to give her a questioning glance. She waved him back to his show and headed into the kitchen.

"As a church mouse," Violet finished stubbornly.

Millie sighed.

"There's definitely something going on," her friend continued. "Sharon talked my ear off about the need for overseeing the government, and pressured me to agree. When I refused to say either way, she got stubborn."

The only light in the kitchen shone from beneath the microwave, casting a homey yellow glow throughout the room. Millie slid into a chair. "What could they be up to?"

"I don't know, but I'm sure it's not good." A pause. "Millie, what side are you on, really?"

"Albert and I are officially neutral. We're both against giving the contract to Little Norm, but I'd never say that publicly. I couldn't hurt Eulie's feelings like that." Something in Violet's question sounded hesitant. "Why do you ask?"

"Oh, nothing."

A long pause, which Millie endured patiently. Normally her friend was quick to speak and quite verbose. When she took her time with words, a great deal of contemplation was going on beneath all those salt-and-pepper curls.

Finally, Violet continued. "What Sharon said kinda made sense. This may have started out being about Little Norm, but it's bigger now. I mean, our City Council *is* made up of regular people. Our neighbors. Shouldn't they have rules about spending tax money?"

It sounded like Hazel and Sharon had been talking.

"I think they do. I mean, they must have." Political discussions, even with her best friend, always left Millie feeling uncomfortable. She *should* know more than she did about her government, should make a point of educating herself. Instead, she was content to cast her vote and let others decide. "Anyway, the mayor leads them. I trust him, don't you?"

"Yes." The answer came without hesitation, and with a hint of relief. "I do trust Jerry."

"And besides," Millie said slowly, thoughts solidifying as she spoke, "if I were making the rules about spending taxpayer money, I would want the Council to do exactly what they're doing. Shop around. Look for bargains."

"Like we do when we're shopping for a new washer and dryer."

"Exactly."

Or a new roof. She glanced over her shoulder, toward the den. *Maybe I will get one or two estimates besides Justin's.*

"And if I were in the market for a new washer and dryer," Violet went on, "I wouldn't limit my shopping to Goose Creek."

Millie chuckled. "If you did, you'd be using a scrub board and stringing a clothesline in the backyard."

"True fact." Violet's laughter sounded lighter than a moment before. "Okay, so unofficially we side with the mayor. Officially, though —"

"We're Switzerland," Millie said.

"Huh?"

She smiled. At least she knew a *little* about politics. "We're neutral," she explained.

"Hey, I like that. We're so Swiss we're full of holes."

"Well, I wouldn't put it exactly like that."

While they shared a final laugh, Rufus waddled into the room. On his way to his corner cushion he paused beside her chair and looked up, a patient request in his eyes. Disconnecting the call, she obliged by rubbing behind his ear. An unpleasant odor wafted toward her. Sniffing her hand, she wrinkled her nose.

"Do you need another bath already?"

One thing about Rufus. He wasn't as slow-witted as Albert claimed. At the dreaded word, he tucked his tail and scurried from the room.

Mayor Jerry Selbo went to bed at eleven o'clock, as usual. When the red digits on the alarm clock read 12:00, he slipped out of bed, taking care not to disturb Cindie.

In the seven years since his entrance into local politics, first with two terms on the Council and then as mayor, he'd never lost sleep over an issue. This water tower situation had taken over his professional life, and now was interfering with his personal life as well.

It'll be over soon.

Though the RFB had just gone out on Friday, they'd already received their first response via e-mail. No one knew it, hopefully. Sally had taken a vow of secrecy, not that she was eager to discuss the water tower with anyone. She hated conflict. If she didn't resign before this was over, he'd be surprised.

I would too, if I thought I could get away with it.

Creeping down the stairs, he stepped over the squeaky fifth step and descended to the main floor in silence. He slipped into the living room, but didn't turn on the light. Normally he would pick up one of his guitars and lose his tension in the music, but he didn't want to wake Cindie. Instead, he headed for his recliner. The house felt stuffy tonight. He detoured to crack open one of the small windows on each side of the large bay window, and stood for a moment breathing in the cool midnight air before sinking into his recliner.

At least there was one benefit from this contentious affair — the decision about making another run for mayor next year had been made for him. The water tower controversy had shot a fatal bullet through his political career. He wasn't sure whether to be upset or relieved.

He must have fallen asleep, because what seemed like moments later he jerked upright. The display on the DVR box read 12:33. What had awakened him? A muffled exclamation. Real, or had he dreamed it?

Hissing whispers from outside drifted through the window. Not a dream, then. Instinct shot him to his feet, but he stood there, hesitant. Should he make a dash for the kitchen phone? Run upstairs and barricade himself and Cindie in the bedroom?

"Shut yer trap, you idjit!"

The words, uttered by a familiar voice, decided him. Keeping to the shadows, he crept closer to the open window. Why in the world was Norman Pilkington slinking around his house in the middle of the night?

"I think I broke something," came the reply. Also familiar. But who?

"Don't tell me I'm gonna hafta carry you outta here, 'cause I ain't a-doin' it."

"Not on me," the second voice said. "One of them garden thingies. I felt it crunch under my boot."

Jerry winced. One of Cindie's garden gnomes had also fallen victim to the water

214

tower controversy.

"Fergit it," Norman commanded. "Heft that there brick."

Brick? Jerry straightened. Time to end this. He turned toward the door, ready to jerk it open and confront the trespassers. A loud *bang!* sounded as something hit the front door, and he nearly jumped out of his skin.

"Dang, Junior! I coulda throwed it better'n that. You plumb missed the whole winder."

Junior Watson. Yes, that was the voice.

"Didn't wanna break the winder. That woulda cost the mayor a bundle to fix."

Norman gave a loud groan. "You really is a idjit. C'mon. Let's git outta here. He'll git the message in the morning."

Jerry followed their progress by the sound of Norman insulting Junior's intelligence. When silence once again settled outside, he opened the front door. An ugly scratch would have to be repaired, but he had extra paint. On the doormat lay a paper-wrapped brick.

Back inside, he flipped on a table lamp. Removing the rubber band, he held the note beneath the lampshade.

Dear Mayor and City Council,
    We ain't about to let you get away with

hiring no outsiders. Come Saturday you'll see we mean business.

Jerry let out a resigned sigh. If the note had been from anyone else, he might have felt threatened. He'd still have to show the sheriff, of course, but only as a precautionary measure. The man couldn't be planning anything too violent or illegal. After all, how could anyone feel threatened when the culprit had signed his note?

Sincerely,
Norman Pilkington, Sr.

DOG COOKIES

1 cup old-fashioned oatmeal
1/3 cup butter
1 1/2 cups boiling water, divided
2 tsp bouillon granules (chicken or beef, depending on your dog's taste)
1 cup sharp Cheddar cheese, shredded
3/4 cup cornmeal
1 beaten egg
2 tsp sugar
3 cups whole wheat flour

Preheat oven to 350° and line a cookie sheet with parchment paper. Combine oatmeal, butter, and 1 cup water. In a separate bowl, combine cornmeal, sugar, 1/2 cup water, bouillon, cheese, and egg. Stir that combination into the oatmeal mixture and blend thoroughly. Add flour a little at a time, stirring to form a stiff dough. Turn onto a floured surface and knead a bit until fully blended. Roll out and cut with squirrel-shaped cookie cutters. (Feel free to use your dog's favorite shapes.) Bake for approximately 40 minutes. Cookies will turn golden brown. Remove parchment paper to counter to cool.

CHAPTER FOURTEEN

An eerie tension settled over Goose Creek.
Being out of town for the better part of each
day, Al only had Millie's word to go on. Her
description of the furtive glances exchanged
by passersby on the streets and the veiled
references to Saturday's mysterious event
made Al almost glad to escape to his job.

Almost.

Thacker made the office more unbearable
than ever. He apparently believed that he
and Al were now buddies since, as he announced to everyone, "We're going to be
fellow geese, flying in the same flock." Most
disturbing of all was his loud and often-
repeated rendition of the theme song from
Mr. Rogers' Neighborhood.

"No!" Al wanted to shout over the cubical
wall. "It is *not* a beautiful day in the neighborhood. And I do *not* want to be your
neighbor."

Saturday arrived with a glorious sunrise,

which Al witnessed from his lounge chair on the back deck. He and Millie wrapped themselves in fleece blankets to ward off the pre-dawn chill and sipped hazelnut coffee while God showed off by splashing color from His shining palette onto a sky full of wispy clouds.

A happy sigh issued from his wife. "Just think, Albert. In a few weeks we'll be sitting on our *verandah* and watching the sunrise over the lake."

"It's a pond," he informed her, "and the *back porch* faces west."

She cast a scowl sideways, and then brightened. "I've been thinking about names for our B&B."

"We're a long way from needing a name."

"I know, but I don't want to keep calling it the Updyke house. How does Woodburn Manor strike you?"

A shudder rippled through him. "The place is an ancient tinderbox. I'd rather avoid any mention of burning wood."

"Good point," she conceded. "How about Beautiful Dreamer B&B?"

"Too cutesy."

"Bluegrass Estates?"

"Too generic."

"What about Lakeview Manor?"

He raised an eyebrow. "There's no lake,

therefore no lake view."

"Don't be an old poop." With an exasperated glance, she burrowed further into her blanket. "What do you suggest?"

"Haven't given it any thought." He cradled the warm mug and regarded the lightening sky. "What about Mother Goose Inn?"

"Albert, be serious."

"I am," he teased. "You could be Mother Goose." A thought occurred to him, and he sobered. "Or maybe Old Mother Hubbard, and we'll have to live in a shoe because the repairs will bankrupt us. What time are we meeting this fellow?"

"Nine-thirty." She twisted around and squinted through the window toward the clock inside. "Just over two hours."

The sun was fully up now, though hiding behind the Andersons' house. Al glowered in that direction. Today he would commit the first of a great many expenditures that posed a threat to his financial security. The bid from the handyman in Frankfort was far less than he'd expected, though he didn't admit that to Millie. He'd be inclined to hire Hinkle based on that alone, regardless of the fact that the other two bids Millie obtained weren't nearly as comprehensive as his. Woody's brother-in-law didn't even bother to inspect the place, but had requested that Millie e-mail him pictures.

Millie was watching him with a pensive expression. "You *will* be nice, won't you?"

His chin jutted forward. "I'm always nice."

After a long blank stare, she burst into laughter. Chuckling, she unwrapped herself from her cocoon and headed for the house. Offended, he did not get up to open the door for her.

Hinkle was already there when they arrived. Though the temperature was still a brisk fifty-one degrees, they'd decided to walk the four blocks. Rufus, putting on a show of obedience for Millie's benefit, trotted sedately alongside them, his nose working overtime to smell every clump of grass growing in the cracks of the long driveway. They approached a motorcycle parked near the front door, chrome gleaming in the bright morning sunlight. A full-face helmet hung from the handle grip. Fascinated, Rufus gave the bike a thorough inspection.

A denim-clad young man rounded the corner of the house, his smile widening when he caught sight of Millie. "Hello ma'am." His gaze switched to Al. "Mr. Richardson, I'm Justin Hinkle."

The guy had a firm handshake and looked Al directly in the eye. A sign of honesty, he'd taught his boys.

"Nice bike." Al gestured toward the motorcycle. "They stopped making the Bad Boy in the mid-nineties, didn't they?"

"That's right. This one's a '96." The young man looked at him with interest. "Do you ride?"

Al shook his head. "I always wanted to, but . . ." He cast a sideways glance at Millie, who managed to look disapproving and friendly at the same time.

Hinkle gave him a sympathetic look, and then, demonstrating a keen sense of diplomacy, changed the subject. "Thanks for meeting me. I wanted to go over a couple of points on the list and make sure I understand the priorities."

"Pretty simple," Al said. "Do only what's necessary, and do it cheaply."

Millie gave him a sharp look. "Expense is a consideration, of course, but we don't want to cut corners if it will affect the quality. We'll be opening a bed and breakfast, so we want things done right."

"Yes, ma'am. I understand." He unlatched a leather sidesaddle on the bike and pulled out a clipboard. Flipping the top sheet over, he ran a finger down the second. "In your e-mail you said the roof is number one. After that, you want me to focus on the kitchen and the back bedroom on the main floor."

"That's right." Millie stretched her neck to glance at his paper. "We want those rooms livable, and then after we move in we'll work on the rest. While we're here, I want to ask you about the window in the back. It's probably easiest to show you."

She pushed the leash into Al's hand and the two of them headed for the backyard. Not about to be left out, Rufus trotted after her, dragging Al behind.

They rounded an overgrown evergreen at the back corner of the house. Before them stretched the vast unkempt lawn leading to the pond. Their arrival startled a herd of squirrels foraging in the grass. Al saw them a split second before Rufus and dropped the leash, thereby avoiding certain injury.

Barking like a crazed creature, the beagle charged toward the nearest rodent. A dozen gray heads rose and squirrels scurried in all directions. Rufus almost overtook the nearest one before it gave a heroic leap and scampered up the knobby bark of a tree. Not deterred in the least, the dog sprinted to the next tree, and then the next, voicing his anger in frenzied woofs and growls. One squirrel, braver or perhaps stupider than the others, paused eight feet up the trunk of a tall oak, turned, and eyed the furious dog, its bushy tail twitching. To Al, it looked like the creature was taunting his would-be attacker.

Watching the show from the sidelines, Hinkle laughed. "That dog sure does hate squirrels, doesn't he?"

Eyeing Rufus with something that came as close to approval as he ever got, Al muttered grimly, "That makes two of us."

They left Hinkle making notes on his clipboard and headed downtown. Though Al typically hung out at Cardwell's on Saturday mornings without Millie, she suggested that, since they were already out, she accompany him.

"Do you mind a short detour?" Millie asked him. "I want to drop by the animal clinic."

Al raised his eyebrows. "Haven't you spent enough time there this week?"

"I want Susan to smell Rufus." Her nose wrinkled as she eyed the oblivious animal trotting along at her side. "It can't hurt, and she could use the business."

Business? Surely she didn't intend to pay good money for the odiferous hound? Doc always did his exams for free. He opened his mouth to voice his objection, but at the rock-hard look she gave him, closed it again. She'd become almost obsessive about the new veterinarian's lack of customers. Besides, twenty or thirty bucks was a mere drop in the deluge that was about to hit their bank account.

The sun had yet to have much effect on the temperature, so the brisk walk to the animal clinic got their blood pumping and warmed Millie to a comfortable level. More traffic than normal traveled Goose Creek's narrow streets. She counted a dozen cars driving down Walnut Street.

An older model green Buick slowed as it approached from behind. The window lowered and Wilma Rightmier leaned out of the car. "You two seen anything yet?"

No need to ask what she meant. Today was Saturday, the day when Whatever-It-Was would happen. That explained the unusual traffic. Half the town had taken to their cars to cruise the streets, hoping to catch sight of something interesting.

Wilma's husband slowed the car even further to keep pace with them as they walked, Rufus trotting happily beside her.

"Nothing so far," she replied to Wilma.

Fred leaned across her lap to address Albert. "We're taking another pass through town and then heading over to Cardwell's for a burger. See you there?"

Albert flipped his hand upward in a noncommittal wave. "Maybe."

Wilma examined Albert for a moment and then smiled at Millie. "See you there."

The car pulled away from them, turned the corner onto Canada Avenue, and disappeared from sight. They walked on a few yards. From the corner of her eye Millie evaluated Albert's expression. His jowls had begun to sag in recent years, which tugged the corners of his mouth into a perpetual scowl. She saw beyond it, of course, but he did appear rather imposing. Perhaps some of that firming cream they advertised on television would help. She would pick some up at the drugstore.

"I wouldn't mind a chicken salad sandwich for lunch," she commented. "Lucy's is the best, next to mine."

He eyed her sideways. "You don't fool me for a minute, Mildred Richardson. Chicken salad is not the issue. You're expecting a spectacle, and you can't stand to miss it."

No sense in trying to duck the issue. She held her head high. "If you don't want to go, I'll have Violet meet me there."

Before he could answer, a high-pitched *toot toot* alerted them to an impending approach. A whir brushed by them on the sidewalk, and a boy's laughter rang in the air as his bicycle sped past. Albert jerked sideways and crashed into her, nearly throwing her off balance. He grabbed for her arm, whether to steady her or himself she wasn't sure, as a second bicycle raced by. Dark, unruly locks waved wildly in the air, stirred by speed and rustled by a lack of exposure to a comb. Rufus, as startled as his owners, filled the air with a canine protest.

Albert cupped his hands around his mouth. "Slow down, you hooligans!"

The second boy turned his head to cast a quick backward glance, and Millie identified the unmistakable features common to the Wainright children.

"Those delinquents are out of control." He followed their progress with a dark glare.

Millie thought of little Willow and her hermit crab. "Their poor mother is overwhelmed trying to support all of them alone. What they need is a man to teach them." She eyed him sideways. "Maybe you could take them under your wing."

The look he gave her stirred up a laugh from deep inside. Her Albert possessed many admirable qualities, but tolerance with children — even his own — was not among them.

When they turned onto Toulouse Street, Rufus suddenly realized where they were. He skidded to a halt and began a nervous pant.

"Come on." She tugged on the leash. "You'll like Dr. Susan. She won't hurt you."

The dog remained unconvinced. She tugged on the leash and he stiffened his legs, forcing her to drag him forward. Adopting the low, firm tone taught by the dog training videos, she commanded, "Rufus, *come.*"

That he knew what she wanted was obvious. That he had no intention of doing so, and was ashamed of his rebellion, was equally obvious. He lowered his head and refused to look her in the eye. No matter how she tugged and jerked, he remained stubbornly in place. Finally, she grasped the leash in both hands and walked backward to drag him down the sidewalk.

A chuckle from Albert drew her attention. He stood to one side, arms folded, and from his expression was thoroughly enjoying the conflict.

She didn't bother to hide her annoyance. "You'll have to carry him."

His laughter faded mid-chuckle. "What? No."

"I can't pull him down the block like this."

She allowed irritation to creep into her voice.

"Sure you can. You're the alpha dog, remember. Show him who's boss."

"The poor thing's clearly terrified. Look at him." Rufus watched them, nose drippy with nerves. "Besides, dragging him over concrete will hurt his paws."

Albert's eyebrows descended, his frown deepening. "I refuse to touch the creature. He stinks."

She couldn't argue with that. "Fine. Then I will."

Stooping, she gathered the rigid animal in her arms and hefted him. Ignoring his whimper, she straightened and staggered a bit before finding her balance. Goodness, Rufus had put on weight lately. Perhaps she should switch to the low-calorie dog food.

With a determined step she marched past Albert, and felt only slightly guilty when, heaving a loud sigh, he reacted exactly as she'd known he would.

"Here, give me the wretched animal before you hurt yourself."

Wretched indeed. After the switch had been made and they continued their trek toward the vet's office, Rufus extended his neck and began a low, mournful keen. Millie half expected an onslaught of animal activists to come running over. Thankfully, they arrived at the clinic without being challenged.

Susan's car occupied a lonely spot in the far corner of the otherwise empty parking lot. Not a good sign for a Saturday, which was typically the clinic's busiest day. She opened the door and ushered Albert and the howling Rufus into the empty waiting room.

The young veterinarian emerged from the back, her expression hopeful. When she recognized Millie, her face fell for only a moment, and then brightened again when her gaze lit on Rufus.

"Hello." She marched toward Albert with an extended hand. "I'm Dr. Susan Jeffries. You must be Mr. Richardson."

"Al," he said, hefting the miserable animal slightly as an excuse for leaving her hand hanging in midair, unshaken.

Susan recovered quickly and turned her attention to the dog. "And this is Rufus. Your mommy has told me all about you."

Millie stopped Albert's eye-roll with a quick glare. "We were out walking and decided to take a chance that you'd be able to, uh —" She glanced at the vacant seats and finished lamely. "— fit him in."

A sardonic expression twisted the girl's

lips. "Yes, well, I think I can make time for him."

"Where's Hazel?" Millie glanced toward the receptionist desk, which looked deserted and a bit forlorn.

"She asked for the day off. Some event she wanted to attend." Susan extended her hand again, this time tentatively, toward Rufus. "And what seems to be your problem today, pup?"

"He stinks." Albert bent over to deposit the dog on the floor, where he stood trembling with his head drooping so that his nose nearly touched the floor. "Positively reeks, in fact. A foul, offensive odor that no amount of bathing eliminates."

While Millie fixed a glare on him, Susan's eyebrows arched.

"Go ahead." He gestured toward the wretched animal. A puddle of drool had collected on the floor beneath his dangling tongue. "Take a good whiff."

Susan dropped onto her knees and reached for Rufus, who stood miserably stiff while she rubbed his head. "There now. I'm not so bad, am I?" She spoke in a low, even tone while she stroked his head and fingered his ears. "I'm just going to look in your ears to see if there's evidence of infection." Gently, she folded one floppy ear over the top of his head and peeked inside. Her features scrunched, nose wrinkling. "He certainly does have an odor."

Albert cast a triumphant glance at Millie. "I'd call it a foul stench."

Now it was her turn to roll her eyes.

"A common reason for bad odor is infection, specifically in the ears." Susan lowered herself to a sitting position beside her patient. "At a glance his appear fine."

"Doc has checked his ears a gazillion times," Millie told her. "They've always been healthy. His teeth too. I've worried it's something he's eating. You know, like when people eat too much garlic and smell like garlic."

"Hmmm." The young woman lifted the dog's front paw and leaned down to sniff it. Her face scrunched and she jerked back. "Oh, my. That's definitely the source."

Millie dropped down beside her boss and sniffed Rufus's paw. His trademark smell slammed into her nostrils so strongly tears stung her eyes. "That's it, all right," she confirmed, climbing to her feet.

"He has stinky feet?" An expression of mild interest crept over Albert's features. Millie restrained herself from pointing out the fact that he shared the trait with their pet.

Susan rubbed a hand over Rufus's back. "People's perspiration can sometimes pick up strong odors from their food. Canines don't sweat like people, but they do secrete an oily substance through their paws and hair follicles. Each animal has its own distinctive odor." She grinned up at them. "As a kid I had a dog whose feet smelled like popcorn."

"So it could be something he's eating?" Millie asked. "But I've tried several different dog foods and nothing seems to make a difference."

"I'd like to run a few tests, just to rule out health issues." With a final caress for Rufus's ears, Susan rose. "Can you bring in a stool sample?"

Millie turned to Albert. "When we get home you can clean up the yard and put some in a baggie. I'll run it back over here."

He fixed her with a look of pure disgust. "I'm not picking up his poop."

Now he was just being obstinate. She planted her hands on her hips. "But you always clean up the yard."

The disgust became utter incredulity. "Mildred Richardson, what are you talking about? I've *never* cleaned up after that animal. That's your job. Always has been."

The man had lost his mind, obviously. "I

did it for a while after I brought him home, but not since then. You're the one who manicures our lawn."

He drew himself up and announced self-righteously. "I draw the line at excrement."

"Well, if you're not cleaning up the poop, and I'm not cleaning up the poop, then who's . . ."

The answer struck them at the same moment. Millie's stomach lurched, while horror crept over Albert's face. They looked down at the culprit, whose ears drooped sorrowfully.

Susan actually chuckled. "No need to look so shocked. Coprophagia is fairly common. There are at least a half-dozen reasons for the behavior. I definitely want a stool sample, and I'll take some blood to check his white count. Do you have time for a thorough exam?"

"Here." Albert thrust the end of the leash toward her. "Keep him. Do whatever you need to fix him."

Millie opened her mouth to protest. She had only intended to ask Susan to take a quick look, not monopolize her clinic time. On the other hand, she certainly didn't have patients lined out the door. And they *definitely* needed help in identifying the reason for this undesirable behavior. "We'll pick him up on our way home. Shouldn't be more than an hour or so."

The young woman gave them a distracted nod, her attention fixed on her patient. When they left, Rufus was too absorbed in misery to do more than cast a tragic glance their way.

Outside, Millie paused on the stoop, face skyward, basking in the sparkling sunlight and a curious sense of lightness. "I feel just like I used to when we left the kids with a sitter for date night."

"I smelled better then." Albert sniffed his hands and grimaced. "Phew. *Eau d' Rufus* is a far cry from Old Spice."

Millie giggled and looped her arm through his. "Come on, Stinky. I'll let you buy me a chocolate malt."

They strolled down the street and joined a trickle of people. Cars lined Main Street in both directions, inching forward, the occupants' eyes scanning all directions. Millie took in the scene with a mounting sense of anticipation. Whatever Norman had planned, he would certainly have an audience.

"Good heavens!" Albert eyed the densely populated sidewalks, a frown gathering on his forehead. "The whole town's here."

A waving hand caught her attention.

"There's Violet."

She waved back and plunged forward, pulling Albert with her. When she caught up with her friend, they retreated to the sidelines and planted their backs against the Freckled Frog Consignment Shop's display window.

"Like ants at a picnic," Violet commented. "They're everywhere."

Millie opened her mouth to agree, but was interrupted by a bellow.

"Bert! Hey Bert. Over here, Bert."

Poor Albert froze, his eyes round as softballs. A tremor rippled through his frame. The resemblance to Rufus was unmistakable, but the misery in his expression stopped her from voicing the comment.

"No," he whispered. "It can't be. Not on a Saturday."

Millie caught sight of a couple approaching at high speed, the man's attention fixed on Albert. It must be the Thackers. *I hope he keeps quiet about our little arrangement.* She glanced at Albert. If he caught wind of their bargain, it would spoil her surprise.

"Look who's here, Sugar Plum. It's my buddy Bert." He pounded Albert on the back, eliciting a pained wince, and then turned on Violet. "And you're Mrs. R. Nice to meet you finally." He shoved an elbow into Albert's ribs, eliciting a wince. "No wonder you keep her hidden. Wouldn't want to let a Hot Mama like her out in public too often. Somebody'll steal her out from under your nose."

Violet's eyebrows disappeared beneath her carefully arranged curls while nearby onlookers cast curious glances in their direction.

Albert seemed to have swallowed his tongue. Vowing to send a framed picture of herself for his cubicle on Monday morning, Millie cleared her voice. "Actually, I'm Millie." She extended a hand toward the woman, whose grin revealed a set of horse teeth that appeared ready to gallop out from her cherry red lips when the starting gun fired. "You must be Mrs. Thacker."

"This isn't my *mother*. She's my wife." Franklin's hee-haw ended in a snort.

"I'm Lulu." The thin woman's frame belied her strength. Millie's hand was crushed and pummeled. "The birth certificate says Luella, but everybody calls me Lulu."

"Except me," put in Franklin. "I call her Sugar Buns." He slapped his wife's behind and they both indulged in a loud chortle.

"Lulu," repeated Millie, struggling to maintain a pleasant expression. "A pleasure to meet you. This is Violet Alcorn. She's your new next-door neighbor."

Millie cast an apologetic look toward her friend, who looked faintly stunned while her hand was similarly abused.

"Violet." Franklin tapped his lips with a finger, eyes skyward while he made a show of contemplating the name. "Reminds me of my favorite fruit. Can I call you Plum?"

Violet turned a blizzardy smile his way. "Not if you expect me to answer."

Both Thackers found that uproariously funny, which drew more stares. Albert's glower had assumed an unmistakable *I told you so* expression. Millie ignored him.

"I'm so glad we got to meet you." She uttered the fib without a qualm, slipping one hand through Albert's arm and grabbing Violet's sleeve with the other. "But we were just heading to lunch, so we'll see —"

"Great idea." Franklin clapped his hands with a noise like a minor explosion. "We'll join you. Maybe you can do some more intros. You know, show off the new geese to the flock."

Millie cast about for an appropriate lie to rescue them from lunch with the Thackers. She had yet to come up with a plausible excuse when a commotion erupted at the far end of Main Street.

A metallic clang reverberated in the air, rendering the onlookers silent. All heads turned toward the end of the block, where a sizable crowd had assembled. The noise turned out to be Junior Watson in possession of a metal trash can lid and a crowbar, which he applied with enthusiasm until Norman stopped him by capturing his arm. Norman whipped a bullhorn from behind his back.

"Attention, Creekers. We'uns are sick to death of bein' ignored. Selbo ain't no more special than the next feller. Now he's set up in a fancy office, he's plumb forgot who put him there. We aim to march around this here street 'til our voices is heard."

The crowd of thirty or so protesters surrounding him gave a cheer. He advanced, flanked by Little Norm and Junior. The others formed a loose line behind them, three or four deep. Some waved signs announcing *Down with Government Tyranny, Our Voices Will Be Heard,* and even *Impeach Mayor Selbo.*

"Look, Sugar Plum." Excitement pitched Franklin's voice high enough to be piercing. "It's a parade!"

Albert turned a disgusted look his way. "It's a protest march."

"I wonder if they'll throw out candy."

Millie instantly forgave Albert for all the negative things he'd ever uttered about Franklin Thacker.

"I'm calling Louise Gaitskill as soon as I get home," muttered Violet.

As the picketers neared, Millie scanned the group. Hazel paced proudly behind Norman, her towering height put to full use in order to hold aloft a sign proclaiming, *Power to the People!* Sharon and Chuck Geddes marched with their heads held high. Edith Boling, her hand wrapped around Boomer's leash, stomped with a militant step heavy enough that Millie half expected the ground to tremble. Even sweet old Delores Brown had joined the protest, scuttling along the perimeter with a stack of flyers which she pressed into the hands of the onlookers. The picketer's combined voices became audible in an off-tune rendition of "We Shall Overcome."

"That must be what they were doing in the barn," Millie told Violet. "Painting signs and rehearsing their song."

"They should have practiced longer."

Overhearing Violet's comment, Franklin let out a guffaw and slapped her on the back. "Good one, Plum! I like you."

Millie shuddered, while Violet's face took on a shade that came close to demonstrating her name. What had she done to her best friend by selling her house to such an odious man?

Shop doors opened on both sides of the street and people spilled out to line the sidewalk. Voices shouted toward the protesters.

"Why don't you go on home, Norman? You aren't accomplishing anything here."

Millie identified Pete Lawson as the heckler. Beside him, his wife, Cheryl, looked mortified.

Junior interrupted their song to shout a reply. "You capitalist pig!" He looked extremely proud of himself for the snappy comeback.

Violet shook her head. "Does he even know what a capitalist is?"

"Probably not," Millie answered.

A grumble stirred among the onlookers while Pete turned as purple as Violet. "Yeah? Well, there's two sides to this issue."

To the obvious amazement of his wife, he whirled and elbowed his way through the crowd to disappear inside Cardwell's. The picketers resumed their song and continued their advance. They had not gotten far before Pete returned, holding a poster board above his head. The message, hastily scrawled in black marker, read *Council Sup-*

porter above a downward pointing arrow. He held the sign high and ran into the street shouting, "Who's with me?"

A surprising number of people rushed to join him. They crossed to the northbound side of Main Street and began their own march in the opposite direction, keeping equal distance as they circled the railroad tracks.

Franklin clapped with glee. "This is great. Which side are you on, Bert?"

Albert's jowls sagged even further, weighed down by disapproval. "Neither. I'm neutral."

The forerunners of Norman's group approached, and Hazel caught sight of them. She pointed a finger in their direction. "Al Richardson, I told you to take a stand. The time has come. What side are you on?"

Every eye in the vicinity swiveled to fix on poor Albert, who looked like he'd just choked on a hornet. Oh, how he hated being the object of attention. Millie's protective hackles rose, and she slipped forward to stand at his side. If he collapsed she doubted if she could catch him, but at least she could break his fall. She leveled a glare at Hazel.

"I . . . I . . ." Face draining of blood, Albert teetered, and Millie slipped an arm around his waist.

From the middle of the procession, Woody shouted, "He supports the Council, and I'll tell you why. He's done the same thing himself. Just hired an out-of-towner to fix up that falling-down old house he's buying, when he shoulda supported Creeker families instead."

A space opened up around them as the surrounding people edged away. Only Violet and the Thackers remained at their sides.

Millie replied with heat and more volume than she intended. "If you mean your brother-in-law, he didn't even bother to look at the house."

Albert turned a horrified gaze her way and hissed, "Don't engage them."

"Probably didn't want anything to do with that catastrophe," Woody called back. "Didn't wanna get killed when the roof collapses."

How dare he! Anger boiling through her veins, Millie's breast heaved and fell as she tried to suck in a calming breath. If people gave his words credence, their bed and breakfast was doomed before it even opened. Nobody would visit a place with a reputation of being unsafe. She shouted a fiery rebuttal. "It's more likely he didn't want to get sued for sloppy workmanship."

Albert stepped in front of her, forcing her

to look away from the odious man. "Mildred Richardson, what are you doing?"

Pulse pounding, Millie drew herself to her full height, which brought her head roughly level with his chin. "I am choosing sides."

Her shout was loud enough to be heard up and down Main Street. Aware that her husband stood gaping after her, she strode forward and stomped through the center of the picketers to the other side of the street.

Chapter Fifteen

"Come on, Rufus." Susan waved the dog cookie in front of the hound's nose. "Your mommy made them, so I'm sure they're yummy."

He turned his head away, expression full of misery. Didn't even sniff the treat, poor thing. Some dogs were like that, terrified of the vet's office. Millie had mentioned that Rufus was a stray, abandoned here and boarded for several weeks before she decided to adopt him. The place probably held frightening memories for him.

Straightening, she returned the cookie to the jar. If she were going to win him over, she'd have to get him out of this place, at least until he relaxed enough to accept her.

"Feel like going for a walk?"

His ears twitched ever so slightly at the word.

"You like walks, huh?" She removed the keys from the pocket of her lab coat and wrapped the end of his leash around her fingers. "We'll just take a quick one up and down the street. Maybe that'll loosen you up a bit."

Sensing his impending departure from the clinic, Rufus perked up. She opened the door, pleased when he trotted obediently outside with her. Key in hand, she lifted it toward the deadbolt.

"Now, give me a second to lo—"

With a jolt that nearly jerked her shoulder out of its socket, Rufus took a flying leap from the porch. The leash flew out of her nerveless fingers while he filled the air with furious barking.

"Come back here!" she shouted.

She might as well have saved her breath. The dog dove toward the lone tree that shaded the parking lot while the object of his pursuit flashed a bushy gray tail as it scampered up the trunk. Rufus screeched to a halt at the base of the tree to deliver a canine bellow. Thank goodness. If she hurried, she could catch him. Leaving her keys dangling from the lock, she bounded off the porch with a leap that would make a long-jumper proud.

Startled, Rufus cast a quick glance at her and then deserted the squirrel. He tore down the sidewalk at top speed.

"Nooo!"

In the past week she could count her patients on two hands. Now one of them was escaping. *Unacceptable.* At least she'd chosen casual shoes over dress pumps this morning. She dug in her heels and sprinted after him.

The crowd closed around Millie, obscuring her from Al's view. He hovered, uncertainty warring with anger in the tense battleground of his stomach. What an infuriating woman. They'd discussed this, had agreed to maintain a nonpartisan stance.

"Well?" demanded Violet, hands planted on her hips. "Are you going to let her go alone?"

That's exactly what he wanted to do. Flee to the solitude of his house, plant himself in a lawn chair on his deck and watch the birds flitter around the bird feeders. But Millie was his wife, his life partner, his soul mate, besides being a sword-sized thorn in his side. Heaving a sigh heavy enough to blow leaves from the trees, he stepped off the sidewalk.

"That's the spirit, man." Thacker's voice rang with approval as he, too, rushed forward, Lulu and Violet on his heels.

I am marching in a protest with Franklin

Thacker.

There were not enough sighs in his body to express his feelings. No possibility that the man would keep mum about this on Monday, either.

Chuck, whom he'd always considered a friend, jeered as he passed. The blazing stare Hazel fixed on him left him smoldering. He sidestepped Old Lady Emerson and dodged past Edith Boling. An eternity later he emerged from the crowd in the center of Main Street and paused to catch his breath on the walkway that connected the north and southbound lanes. The railroad tracks lay beneath his feet, and before him the rapidly expanding group of protesters who trailed behind Pete's hastily made sign. No going back now.

A commotion to his right drew his attention. Speeding down the center of the tracks in his direction were two bicycles, the mop-headed boys standing to pedal as fast as they could over the uneven track. A brown blur raced after them, trailing a bright blue rope. No, a leash. Al did a double take. Was that Rufus?

Bringing up the rear was a red-faced Susan, arms pumping, the tails of her lab coat flapping behind her.

The protest song died and the march was

temporarily suspended as everyone paused to watch the spectacle of the town's new veterinarian galloping down the train tracks in pursuit of a canine escapee. She stumbled, and an audible gasp rose from both sides. At that speed a fall would certainly prove disastrous. Her recovery elicited a relieved sigh from the onlookers, but she'd lost precious ground. Rufus pulled ahead.

Al stepped backward seconds before the Wainright boys whizzed past, shrieking with glee. Rufus didn't even pause as he, too, darted by. Susan, her gaze focused on the object of her pursuit, probably wasn't even aware that she commanded the attention of the entire town.

Thacker's laughter, punctuated by snorts, rose into the air. He slapped his thighs with both hands. "What a great town," he shouted, wiping tears from his eyes. "We're going to love it here."

Searching the crowd in front of him, Al found Millie. She stood with hands covering her face, shaking her head.

Her surroundings a blur, Susan drew on reserves of strength she didn't know she possessed. A burst of speed gained her an advantage, and Rufus's leash bounced across the train tracks in front of her, a mere yard away. He was tiring, no doubt due to an extra ten pounds of table scraps she suspected he was fed. If she could . . . just . . . reach . . .

A figure appeared in her peripheral vision. One part of her brain registered the fact that it was a man, and that he ran at a diagonal path that would intersect hers in a few seconds.

"Grab him!" She intended to yell, but breath failed her and the words emerged in a raspy whisper.

Denim and brown hair sped past and, with the agility of an athlete, the man bent and scooped up the leash without missing a stride.

"Whoa there, fella."

The deep voice rumbled from a well-muscled chest. He tugged the dog to a stop, and bent to scrub at his ears. Rufus collapsed on the worn toes of a pair of black leather boots, sides heaving. Breath coming in ragged heaves, Susan bent over, hands resting on her thighs, and willed herself not to throw up. When she straightened, she looked directly into the intoxicating gaze of Justin Hinkle.

"Here you go, ma'am." He flashed a disarming smile as he pressed the leash into her hand.

"Th— Th—" She gulped and tried again. "Thank you."

"He must have gotten away from you."

A fresh explosion erupted in her face. "It happened so quickly. One minute he was standing beside me and the next, he nearly jerked my arm off."

Concern carved tiny lines at the corners of his eyes. "I hope you weren't hurt." He took her hand, gentle fingers exploring her wrist.

Rational thought fled, and her world was reduced to a three-foot radius, with the electrifying warmth of Justin's touch forming the center.

The moment ended abruptly when a cluster of people arrived, their feet kicking up gravel.

"Oh my. I am so sorry. Bad dog, Rufus. Bad."

Susan tore her gaze away from Justin's ocean-blue depths to fix on a familiar face. Millie, accompanied by her husband and three people she didn't know. With a start, she realized Justin still held her hand. She snatched it away and shoved it into her coat pocket.

"It's not his fault," she assured Millie. "I should have kept a tighter grip on the leash.

He was frightened, and there was a squirrel."

Al nodded as though that explained everything, and settled an almost approving glance on the dog.

A wide grin erupted on the lean-faced man beside him. "That was quite a show you put on, gal. Just what we needed, too. Things were getting a little tense."

"Show?" For the first time, her surroundings registered. Why were all these people standing around in the street? And staring at her?

They'd all seen her mad dash after Rufus. Her vision blurred, and she wavered on her feet.

Justin steadied her with a strong hand around her arm. "Maybe you ought to sit down for a bit."

She shook her head, cheeks on fire. "No, I've got to get back to the clinic. I left the keys in the door." Glancing at Millie, she bit down on her lower lip. "I'll understand if you don't trust me to take Rufus."

Without a moment's hesitation, Millie covered the hand holding his leash with both of hers. "Of course I trust you. You're an excellent veterinarian." She said the last in a voice loud enough to carry into the surrounding crowd.

"Mind if I tag along?"

With a start, she looked at Justin. Did he think she couldn't handle the dog? "Why?" A hint of suspicion crept into her voice.

He lifted a shoulder and held her gaze with a smile that melted her insides. "Because I want to."

Tongue delightfully numb, the only reply she could manage was a nod.

The veterinarian and the handyman sauntered off, an exhausted Rufus in tow. Al grabbed Millie's arm. "Come on. We're going home."

Stubborn to the core, that was his Millie. Her entire body stiffened and her lips pursed to form a determined bow. "I'm staying."

"Me too." Violet stepped up beside her, shoulder-to-shoulder in a show of solidarity.

"C'mon, Bert. Let's pound a bit of pavement." Thacker actually extended a finger and poked Al's stomach. "The exercise will do you good, buddy."

A dozen replies clogged his throat, vying for airspace. Before anything emerged, the pro-council contingent arrived, crossed the tracks in front of Al, and continued southward at the same time the protesters crossed over at the far end of the block. Casting a defiant stare his way, Millie joined the troop.

He stared after her. Why couldn't they just go home? Leave this madness to others and return to the peace of his house and yard and back deck. Only they were no longer his, and the town he loved would never again be the harmonious retreat he looked forward to five days each week. He lifted an angry glare toward the object that started this whole thing. The nauseous-colored water tower stood sentinel over Main Street, blithely unaware of the commotion going on below.

Shoulders drooping, Al followed his wife.

A cold breeze kicked up, as though Old Man Winter wasn't quite ready to concede the year to spring. Al raised his collar and huddled within the scant protection of his jacket. At least while they headed south it was at their backs. Perhaps he could convince Millie to abandon the cause at the end of the street.

The shriek of a siren cut through the air, and the jeers and catcalls from both sides fell silent. He turned to see a row of police cruisers rounding the corner. Two headed in his direction while two veered off, crossed the tracks, and drove south on the north-bound side of the street, blue lights flashing, to intersect the other mob.

Protesters on both sides halted mid-stride to watch their progress. The first cruiser rolled to a stop a few feet in front of Norman. Since he'd been bringing up the rear and everyone had turned, Al found himself in the uncomfortable position of being at the front of the pro-council group and staring through the windshield into the unsmiling face of a deputy.

Car doors opened, and uniformed officers emerged from all four vehicles. From their heavy belts dangled a variety of official-looking paraphernalia, most menacing of which was a pistol.

Millie stepped up from behind and slid beneath his arm. He avoided the obvious comment, that if she'd left when he wanted they would be nearly home now instead of facing a heavily armed squadron of stern-faced lawmen.

The grimmest of the four paced toward Norman. His voice carried easily down the silent block. "Folks, you're gonna have to disperse. Go on home." His glance slid across the street and landed on Al, who did his best to appear unofficial and harmless. "All of you."

Norman held his ground, his stare full of defiance. "We'uns are exercisin' our rights as American citizens. It's still a free country, ain't it?"

Sheriff Grimes, whose face Al recognized from a billboard at the county line last November, planted his feet. "Yes, sir, it is. But this is an illegal demonstration."

Murmurs stirred among protesters and observers alike. Delores issued a tiny shriek of dismay and dropped her flyers, which were picked up by a blast of wind and skittered across the road like confetti. Junior retreated a half-step, leaving Little Norm and his father as the clear frontrunners.

"Ain't neither," Norman insisted.

"May I see your permit?" the sheriff asked politely.

Uncertainty descended on the older man. "Permit?"

"Yes, sir. Demonstrations of this type require a permit. Besides, you are blocking a public street."

A familiar figure emerged from the passenger side of the sheriff's car. Mayor Selbo rounded the front bumper to stand beside Grimes.

Norman gathered his full height and stabbed a finger in Selbo's direction. "I shoulda knowed you was behind this." He whirled and addressed his followers. "Now you'uns see what we've got runnin' this town. Cain't keep any kind of Creeker business in Goose Creek without callin' in outsiders."

Now it was Grimes's turn to bristle. "I am an elected official in this county, and therefore not an outsider."

"If you don't live in the Creek, you ain't a Creeker," replied Norman.

"Norman, listen to me." Selbo raised his voice to address the entire crowd. "Everyone, listen to me. Your voices have been heard. Once this issue has been resolved, I will personally review the established procedures for the expenditure of public funds, and I'll arrange a town meeting to explain them. If a majority of the voters believes they need to be changed, the council will draft new ones." He straightened, and a glint of steel crept into his normally easygoing manner. "As for the current issue, the Council strongly believes we are handling the situation in a fair and equitable manner."

"The Council?" Hazel's voice held equal amounts of derision and defiance.

The mayor held her gaze steadily. "Yes, the people duly elected to provide leadership and direction for Goose Creek. Some of whom are huddled in their homes right now, afraid to come out in public and face their fellow residents. Half-afraid to send their children to school because of the taunts they've experienced in the past few days." His tone turned bitter. "If that was your aim, then you've succeeded."

The militant expression on Hazel's face faded, and Al spied more than a few lowered heads.

"So you said you's gonna be fair." Norman squinted up at the man. " 'At mean Little Norm's gonna get the job?"

A heavy silence descended on both sides of the street. Breaths were held collectively.

Selbo answered without flinching. "It means Little Norm's bid will be evaluated the same as everyone else's. If the Council decides his is the most effective use of taxpayer money, he will get the job."

"That's fair," shouted Pete from somewhere behind Al.

Several heads across the street turned to glare, but others appeared uncertain.

Norman glowered, clearly not convinced of his son's chances. Little Norm returned to his side and placed a hand on his shoulder. Though he spoke quietly, Al had no trouble hearing him. "C'mon, Pa. Let's go home. I might need your help with that bid."

Apparently unconvinced, Norman stood his ground and indulged in a stare-off with the mayor.

"I'll help too," announced Hazel, and several heads nodded.

Others sidled away as the crowd began to disburse. Junior slipped away, and even bent to scoop up a handful of discarded leaflets on his way. Soon only a few people stood behind Norman.

"I still say you'uns ain't worth a hill a beans, and if 'n you brings an outsider in here, you'll be sorry."

Sheriff Grimes folded his arms across his chest. "Are you threatening a public official, sir?"

The little man didn't have a chance to answer. Little Norm physically pulled his father back and, perhaps sensing he'd crossed a line, Norman went willingly. The few protesters who stood behind him parted to let the pair pass.

"Well, that was fun." Thacker clapped his hands and then rubbed them together. "Now, how about that lunch, Bert?"

Al discovered that he could reply, quite truthfully, that he had entirely lost his appetite.

CHAPTER SIXTEEN

Millie could hardly wait to get to work on Monday morning.

"So, how did it go?" she asked as she bustled through the front door.

Susan turned from straightening the dozen or so magazines on the wall rack in the Kuddly Kitties room. "The blood tests all look normal, and the cultures are negative. But I have a shampoo I'd like you to try."

Millie paused in the act of sliding a tray of cookies onto the reception counter. She blinked, momentarily at a loss. Then she realized.

"Not Rufus. I meant with Justin."

"Oh." The girl turned away and adjusted the top rack again. "Fine. He seems like a nice guy."

Her sudden nonchalance could have a couple of meanings. Had they not hit it off as well as expected? When Millie and Al picked up Rufus on the way home Saturday things seemed to be going very well between the two of them, with enough sparks flying that even Al, who was typically clueless, noticed them. That meant either Justin had not asked her out and Susan was fretting, or he had asked and she wanted the date to remain private.

Not deterred by the latter reason, Millie adopted her best I'm-a-friendly-ear-tell-me-everything manner. "So are you planning to see him again?"

"No." The answer came quickly. "He asked me to dinner on Tuesday, but I said no."

"Why on earth did you do that?"

A flush arose on the girl's cheeks, and for a moment Millie thought she'd overstepped a boundary. But then Susan answered.

"I said yes initially, but then I talked it over with Daddy. We agreed that this isn't a good time for me to date. I've just opened a business." Her hands indicated the room. "It'll take all my attention if it's going to succeed. Beginning a relationship right now would be a distraction. So I texted Justin yesterday and told him I couldn't go."

Her eyes didn't quite meet Millie's, which said a lot. Millie set her teeth and swallowed an unflattering observation about apron strings and when they should be cut. Instead she managed to utter, "I see."

Susan flashed her a quick look. "He's totally right. I agree with him completely. And besides, I do my laundry on Tuesdays."

With difficulty, Millie maintained a blank expression. Mind grasping for a response that wouldn't get her fired on the spot, she grabbed the tray and held it aloft. "Look what I brought. Chewy chocolate cookies."

The veterinarian's face lit, either because of the cookies or in relief for an end to the uncomfortable conversation. She inspected the goodies eagerly. "Can I have one?"

"Take several," Millie advised. "They won't last long once the day's appointments start arriving."

A sour expression settled on Susan's face. "If we have any at all after Saturday's fiasco."

"Oh, I think we will. You certainly got a personal introduction to the entire town. And you know what they say. No advertising is bad advertising."

"I hope you're right." Susan bit into a cookie and closed her eyes in pure enjoyment. "Oh, these are heavenly. Maybe I'll take a couple into the back, in case you're right."

She loaded her hands and, with a grateful

smile, headed for her office. The door had not even finished swinging before Millie snatched up her purse to fish for Justin's phone number.

"It's a bad decision, Millie." Al pitched his voice low as he spoke into the phone. No doubt Thacker sat on the other side of the cubicle wall straining to hear. He swiveled his chair to face the opposite direction. "Nobody in their right mind would pay for work on a house that isn't theirs."

"But it *will* be ours soon. The closing date is just over three weeks away, and we'll need to move in that weekend."

Al shut his eyes at the reminder. Another argument he'd lost. Who knew Thacker would have enough cash to pay for the house without a mortgage and insist on moving quickly? His efforts to stall the closing date had failed in the face of Millie's steely enthusiasm.

"If we wait to fix the roof until after the closing," Millie said, "we'll have to put all our stuff in storage and rent an apartment. We might even have to sign a lease. It makes much more sense to move directly into the Manor and save that money."

"The Manor?"

She gave a self-conscious laugh. "Well, we

have to call it something."

Swallowing a comment about settling such a grand name on an ancient money pit, he replied instead, "But what if the deal falls through? We can't afford to lose that kind of money."

"Louise and I talked about that. She's going to contact the Updykes and ask if they'll agree to reimburse us if that happens."

She's thought of everything. He slumped in his chair. "All right. If they say yes, then I guess we can go ahead with it. Call Hinkle and see when he can get started."

"I did. He's coming tomorrow to take measurements and pick up a check for the deposit. Oh, here comes a patient. Gotta run. Love you."

Al sat holding the dead receiver. This morning he'd begun the process of withdrawing money from his investments. When he pressed the Enter key, a sick flutter erupted in his stomach. Now that flutter morphed into a somersaulting heave. This was real. There was no stopping the sale now. He felt like he'd been strapped to the front of a steam engine, and his beloved wife was shoveling coal into the boiler as fast as she could.

Thacker's head popped up above the cubicle wall. "Speaking of roofs, how old is the one on my new house?"

If the phone receiver had been made of glass, it would have shattered in Al's hand.

To Susan's relief, Millie's prediction proved true. Tuesday was the busiest day since Doc left for Florida. Not a single cancellation, and three people called to ask if she had time to squeeze their animals in. Plus four new patients made appointments for later in the week.

Maybe Daddy and I won't go bankrupt after all.

She scribbled the diagnosis code on Precious's chart and handed the paper to the Maltese's owner. "Here you are, Mrs. Easterly. Give that to Millie, and ask her to schedule a follow-up appointment for next week." She stroked the dog's silky fur. "I think Precious's eye infection will clear up by then, but I want to make sure."

"Thank you, Dr. Susan."

The woman gathered the little dog into her arms while Susan held the door open. She stopped in the doorway, a grin creeping onto her face.

"I was in town on Saturday, you know."

Susan bit back a groan. *Was there anyone in Goose Creek who* wasn't *there?* "Oh?"

"You sure can run." The grin widened.

"I'll bet you were a runner in college, weren't you?"

"High school," she said for the fifth time that day. "400 meter relay."

"I knew it!" She nuzzled Precious. "You won't be outrunning Dr. Susan, you slow thing."

Susan followed them down the short hall and swung open the door to the reception area. Mrs. Easterly passed through, explaining to Precious how she couldn't possibly be expected to catch the birds she loved to chase because her legs were too short. Susan opened her mouth to say goodbye, and then glimpsed the man standing in front of Millie's desk. Her jaw dangled, words frozen in her throat.

Justin caught sight of her, and his eyes erupted with sparkles. "Susan."

How did he manage to make her name sound exotic and glamorous? Even more curious, why did she long to hear him say it again, and again?

Swallowing against a dry throat, she managed to reply in a reasonably calm tone. "What are you doing here?"

Mrs. Easterly turned a surprised glance toward her, and Millie, seated behind the reception counter, arched her eyebrows. Obviously, her tone wasn't as calm as she thought.

"What I mean is, uh, I didn't expect to see you here. Or anywhere. Since you live in Frankfort, that is." She snapped her mouth shut before her babbling got worse.

Millie took the paper from Mrs. Easterly's hand. "He's here to see me."

"Oh." Disappointment flooded her. She had assumed he was there to try to convince her to keep their date tonight. A stupid assumption, since she knew Millie had hired him.

She started to retreat but Justin hurried around the reception counter, aqua eyes fixed on her face. "But I really hoped I'd run into you. Matter of fact, I plan to hang around until you finish for the day and try to convince you to change your mind." His expression became pleading. "Have dinner with me."

A pleasant warmth washed over her. "I really can't —"

"Oh, come on. We'll grab a quick burger or something." He raised two fingers like a boy scout making a pledge. "I promise to have you home in time to do your laundry."

Those eyes would be the downfall of her resolve. The longer she looked into them, the less sense her decision to cancel their date made. What harm was there in dinner with a friend? A girl had to eat, didn't she?

"Welllllllll . . ." Indecision gave the word a few extra syllables.

He straightened, grinning. "Great. When will you be finished here?"

Before she could answer, Millie piped up. "Your last appointment is at three forty-five."

"I'll be here by four thirty," he said.

Susan started to ask if they could make it five so she could go home and change clothes, but he stopped her by raising a finger in the air. "No backing out." Before she could voice her question, he whirled and dashed through the door.

"He seems like a nice young man," commented Mrs. Easterly. "And quite pleasant to look at, too."

Millie nodded and typed the diagnosis code into the computer. A secretive smile curved the receptionist's lips, giving her the look of someone who was particularly pleased with herself.

MILLIE'S CHEWY CHOCOLATE COOKIES

2 sticks butter, room temperature
2 cups sugar
2 eggs
2 tsp vanilla extract
3/4 cup unsweetened cocoa powder
2 cups flour
1 tsp baking soda
1/2 tsp salt

Preheat oven to 350°. Cream butter and sugar together. Add eggs and vanilla, stirring until well combined. Sift the dry ingredients together and add to creamed mixture a little at a time. Form a rounded spoonful of cookie dough into a ball and place it on a baking sheet lined with parchment paper, pressing slightly to form a disc. Bake in preheated oven for approximately 10 minutes. Cool slightly on cookie sheet before removing parchment paper with cookies to the counter to continue cooling.

CHAPTER SEVENTEEN

A dozen times during the afternoon Susan picked up her phone to text Justin and cancel the date. All Daddy's reasons still held true. The business needed her full attention if it were to have a chance to succeed. Every effort should focus on that end. The list of former patients she had painstakingly assembled awaited phone calls, which she could make while her laundry was in the wash. She ought to call Daddy so he could act as the voice of reason and talk her out of spending the evening with Justin.

But whenever she reached for the phone something stopped her, and the call to Daddy never got made. Instead, she ran home during a lull in the schedule to grab a change of clothes. Leggings instead of a skirt, since Justin made a point of saying he intended to wear jeans, but she could at least wear heels and a pretty top. And makeup.

At 4:10 she said goodbye to Mrs. Penny-weather and her tabby cat — with only five toes on each foot, imagine that! — and closed herself in the bathroom. She studied the image in the vanity mirror. Goodness, was the light dim in here or did she really look that washed-out? She should start wearing makeup every day. And her hair . . . she pulled the ponytail holder out and shook her head. What a limp, mousy mess. She rummaged in the bag she'd brought from home and extracted a long-ignored curling iron. Hopefully she could remember how to use the thing.

Twenty minutes later she stepped back and examined the transformation. Not bad. Decent, in fact. Gentle curls falling around her face definitely softened the sharp angles of her jaw. And her skin took on a silky appearance with a touch of powder. Yes, a definite improvement from the shoulders up. If only the mirror showed the rest of her. She whirled once, enjoying the silky feel of the swirling gossamer fabric. The long top settled around her trim thighs. Looking down, the effect was flattering. Hopefully Justin thought so.

She emerged, the heels of her strappy sandals clicking on the hallway floor when she stowed the bag in the office. The sound of the clinic's front door closing and the rumble of a deep male voice set off a violent flutter in her stomach. For a moment her confidence failed and she sagged against the edge of her desk. What was she doing? She hadn't had a date since her freshman year in college. Her studies were too important, Daddy advised, and he'd been right. Then veterinary school absorbed every spare minute. The effort had been worth it. She'd emerged at the top of her class.

I'm stalling.

Stiffening her spine, she strode toward the reception area.

If she'd had any doubts about her looks, they evaporated when she came through the clinic door. Justin stopped his conversation with Millie mid-sentence. His gaze swept her from head to foot and back again, coming to a stop on her eyes. Admiration radiated from him in nearly palpable waves.

"Wow. You look . . ." He finished his sentence with a long whistle.

Heart pounding, she lowered her gaze. "Thank you."

"What a beautiful tunic, dear." Millie's voice bubbled with enthusiasm. "So flattering. And that hairstyle really suits you." The receptionist gazed at her with something approaching maternal pride, which brought a pleasurable warmth to Susan's cheeks.

"Uh, there's only one problem," Justin said.

Her gaze flew upward. "Problem?"

"Do you have anything sturdier that covers your toes?" A frown gathered on his forehead as he peered at her sandals. "Leather boots, or even tennis shoes would be better than those."

"You don't like them?" Horrified, she heard a quiver in her voice.

"Sure I do." He took two giant strides forward and touched her arm. "They're great, really. But they're not safe on a motorcycle."

Now it was her turn to stand with her mouth gaping.

"You're on your motorcycle?" Millie stood to look out the window. Consternation creased her brow. "You can't take a date on a motorcycle."

His head cocked sideways. "Why not? I brought an extra helmet."

Millie heaved an exasperated sigh. "A motorcycle isn't appropriate for a first date."

Justin looked truly perplexed. "But it's a Harley."

The answer was so outlandish Susan couldn't hold back a laugh. She'd heard that Harley Davidson owners were proud, but she'd never actually met one. The bewildered expression he turned on her made her laugh even harder.

"What's funny about a Harley?" he asked, sounding slightly offended.

She answered with more laughter. The situation really wasn't that funny, but her mirth was fed by pent-up nerves, and she couldn't stop. What would Daddy say when he found out she'd gone on a date with a biker? *And* that she'd ridden on his motorcycle? She bent double, laughing, and then recovered enough to say, "Just give me a minute to change shoes."

"If you have any sturdier pants you might want to put them on too." At her questioning glance, he explained, "If a bug hits your leg at sixty miles an hour, it's gonna hurt like heck unless you have some sort of protection."

Her lips twitched at the idea of projectile insects, but she controlled herself as she returned to her office to change back into the slacks and T-shirt she'd worn beneath her lab coat.

"That little guy was born at the beginning of February." Susan followed Justin's nod to a nursing colt at the far end of the pasture. "I was driving by the day they turned him out for the first time, so I pulled off to watch and struck up a conversation with the breeder. They say he has the look of his sire, who was a Derby winner. Sometimes I come out here just to watch him."

When they left the animal clinic Justin took her to a roadside diner down a tree-lined country road, the kind of place she would never have the nerve to visit on her own. The tiny building could use a good painting, and the sign hung slightly lopsided. Inside they'd sat at one of the five tables, where Susan was served the best burger she'd ever eaten, smothered in grilled onions and dripping with cheese. They talked for almost two hours, the server refilling their glasses with sugary sweet tea more times than she could count. Then he drove her down the narrow country lane beneath a canopy of tender spring leaves that seemed somehow closer and more alive from the back of a motorcycle than they ever did in a car.

Now they stood in the grass at a white plank fence surrounding a peaceful green pasture where a half-dozen foals and mares grazed in the deep green Kentucky grass. On the horizon sat a gigantic white barn with blue trim, covered in cross-hatched doorways and topped with a trio of spire-style cupolas. Though the farms around her home in southwestern Kentucky had their share of traditional horse barns, she had never seen so many gorgeous and extravagant thoroughbred barns as graced the central part of the state.

The colt lifted its head and stood for a moment beside the mare, then took off across the grass with the frolicking gait of a foal that has not yet grown into its long legs. Susan climbed up onto the bottom plank and hung her arms over the top of the fence to get a better look. "He's going to be a runner."

"You know it. I'm not a betting man, but if he makes it to the Derby in a couple of years I might have to make an exception." His expression as his gaze followed the colt held a paternalistic touch of pride.

A few minutes later Justin held out a hand to help Susan down. When she stood firmly on the grass, he did not release her but instead entwined his fingers in hers, which set off a delicious tickle in her stomach as they covered the few steps back to the waiting motorcycle. When they arrived, it was with obvious reluctance that he let go so he could help her shrug into the bulky leather jacket he insisted she wear. His hands lingered on her shoulders a minute longer than absolutely necessary, and she didn't mind in the least.

"What do you think of your first ride on a motorcycle?"

"I love it. It feels so . . ." She threw her arms wide as though to embrace the countryside. "So freeing."

"You're a convert." Approval sparkled in his eyes. "Before you know it you'll be shopping for your own."

A laugh emerged at the idea. Daddy would have a conniption. She shook her head. "I'd much rather be a passenger. That way I don't have to worry about shifting gears or traffic or all that stuff. I can sit back and enjoy the view."

He grinned. "When I was little and rode on the back of my dad's bike I used to sing at the top of my lungs. Inside the helmet nobody could hear me."

Speaking of helmets — which Justin insisted were mandatory — reminded Susan of her hair. In the restroom of the diner she'd been horrified at the image that stared back at her from the mirror. So much for her efforts with the curling iron. Her hair plastered against her skull, the ends that hung beneath the full-face helmet ratty with tangles from being whipped by the wind. A comb took care of the snarls but could do nothing to coax body into the lifeless locks.

She raked her fingers through her hair. "Next time I think I'll bring a baseball cap. When the helmet comes off, the cap goes on."

His fingers paused in the act of zipping his jacket and his eyes locked on to hers. Her breath lodged in her chest. Completely unable to look away, she stood still as his hand rose to tuck a strand of hair behind her ear.

"Next time." His deep voice rumbled just above a whisper. "Lady, I like the way you think."

Susan's heart was still tap-dancing when she climbed onto the motorcycle behind him and wrapped her arms around his waist.

The sun had almost set when they turned the corner onto Susan's street to find a commotion in progress. Her first thought was that Saturday's demonstration had re-surged, but why would anyone want to picket Walnut Street? Flashing blue lights reflected off houses and the faces of a dozen or so onlookers gathered on the sidewalk. A second later she identified the house where the commotion took place, and her pulse accelerated. The police car was parked in the Hunsakers' driveway, the crowd gathered beside their mailbox.

Oh no! Has something happened to Mr. or Mrs. Hunsaker?

Her arms tightened around Justin as he steered the bike down the street. Heads turned, and every eye fixed on them as he rolled to a stop by the curb. Justin hopped off and turned to help her.

She jerked the helmet off. "What's wrong? Has something happened to the Hunsakers?"

As the question left her tongue she noticed a trio on the front porch. A deputy sheriff holding a clipboard and pen stood beside her worried-looking landlords.

Mrs. Hunsaker caught sight of her. Concern fled her face and she pointed at Susan. "There she is!"

The woman bounded down the porch steps and practically ran across the lawn to gather Susan in a bone-crushing embrace. "Thank the Lord you're okay. We've been so worried."

Stunned, Susan endured the hug with her arms hanging at her side. She looked at Justin, who appeared as clueless as she.

"I'm fine," she told her landlady. "Why wouldn't I be?"

The deputy and Mr. Hunsaker arrived then, the crowd retreating a few yards at their approach.

"Are you Susan Margaret Jeffries?" the officer asked.

What in the world had she done wrong? Her mind skipped across the last few days and came up empty. She'd done nothing illegal. Always drove the speed limit, came to a full stop at intersections, used her turn signals faithfully.

Swallowing, she nodded as Justin stepped to her side and placed a supportive arm around her shoulders. "I'm Susan Jeffries. Is there a problem?"

The deputy's gaze shifted to Justin and his eyes narrowed. "Are you all right, ma'am? Not being held against your wishes, or compelled to do anything you don't want to do?"

Now it was Justin's turn to look shocked. A flicker of suspicion erupted in her brain. *No. He wouldn't.*

"I'm fine," she told the officer. "Why would you ask that?"

"You've been reported as missing, ma'am. Possibly kidnapped."

An excited rumble erupted among the onlookers. Mrs. Hunsaker sagged against her husband.

"Kidnapped?" Justin choked on the word. "I didn't kidnap her. We've been on a *date.*"

Humiliation blazing in her face, Susan could only nod in agreement. Not the slightest doubt who was responsible. *I can't believe he did this.*

The officer expelled a breath. "We're all relieved to hear that, Miss Jeffries."

"Dr. Jeffries," Mr. Hunsaker corrected. "She's a veterinarian."

Several of the spectators gazed at her with renewed interest.

"*Dr.* Jeffries." The deputy addressed the observers. "Everything's fine here, folks. Dr. Jeffries has been on date."

A smattering of applause met the announcement and a groan rose in Susan's throat. Her first date in years, and the event earned her a standing ovation. And this after a lunatic dash down Main Street in pursuit of an escaped patient.

The officer raised his clipboard and clicked open his pen. "I'll need a statement from the both of you. Shouldn't take but a minute or two. After that you might want to call your father, ma'am. Let him know you're okay."

Completely mortified, Susan could only nod.

She paced the length of her tiny combination living and bedroom, gripping her phone in a hand that still trembled with humiliation. "Why would you do that, Daddy?"

"Because I was worried. Here I am, two hundred fifty miles away, and my little girl stops answering her phone. Texts too. You always answer when I call. What am I supposed to think?"

He *did* sound worried. Guilt stabbed at her, dulling the edge of her frustration. He had a point. Even when she was working, if she couldn't take a call she would send a text saying she'd get back to him when she could.

"I would have called as soon as I saw your missed calls." Twelve of them, and twice as many texts with messages of escalating panic. The guilt knife twisted in her gut.

"How was I to know that? You never forget your phone. It's completely out of character."

True. She even kept her cell phone in her lab coat pocket while she worked. As soon as she realized she'd left it at the clinic she should have asked Justin to turn around so she could retrieve it, but talking was impossible while zooming down a country road on the back of a motorcycle. She'd run over to the clinic to retrieve it after the police left.

"Something else that's out of character is

your behavior tonight. I thought we'd decided that you weren't going out with this boy."

Not a boy. Justin is all man. She indulged in a dreamy smile and kept the comment to herself. "It wasn't planned. He came to the clinic this afternoon and offered to buy me a hamburger."

"And that took three and a half hours?"

"We went for a ride in the country afterward." She allowed a touch of defiance to creep into her voice. "I had a good time. Is that so bad?"

"Of course not. Everyone's entitled to a little enjoyment in life." A pause, and when he continued his tone held a note of resignation. "Tell me about him. Where did he go to school?"

"The University of Kentucky." A truthful answer. No need to tell Daddy that Justin dropped out during his sophomore year to work construction.

"Good school." His voice was guarded. "What's his profession?"

Though she adored her father, Susan knew he tended to be something of a white collar snob. She paced to the corner and peered into Puff's aquarium. "He, uh, owns his own business."

"Doing what?"

She hesitated. Justin's business name, *Hinkle the Handyman,* would put her father off for sure. "He's a subcontractor, and licensed in several areas."

"A subcontractor? Do you mean he's a construction worker?" Disbelief colored his tone.

"More like a builder," she hurried to say. "He specializes in repairs, and has an electrician's license too."

A long pause ensued, during which Daddy drew in a slow breath. "Sweetheart, what are you doing? You've worked so hard to get to where you are. You've got to keep your head about you, now more than ever."

"I will." She turned at the window and paced four long steps in the opposite direction, ending at the dinette table. "It was only a hamburger. One date can't possibly pose a threat to my future."

"*Our* future," he commented. "After all, if you become distracted to the point that your business fails, I'll be forced to pick up the bank note."

Deflated, she dropped onto the futon that did double duty as sofa and bed. She must never forget Daddy's role as principle financier in the Goose Creek Animal Clinic. Without him, she could never have bought her business.

Nor could she ignore his warning, not with a good conscience. Justin Hinkle could definitely become a dangerous distraction.

CHAPTER EIGHTEEN

Saturday arrived, but not a tranquil Saturday of days gone by. The house had been transformed, and Al didn't like it one bit. The contents of his once-peaceful abode had exploded off the walls and shelves and drawers to lie in cluttered piles all over the house, waiting to be packed into the collapsed boxes that had taken over his garage. Moving day loomed on the horizon, a mere two weeks away. Correction. Thirteen days. Millie had created a countdown with red ink on the kitchen calendar, so there was no ignoring the fact. He wandered from room to room, scuffling in his slippers around the chaos. Perhaps he might go to the office for a few hours of order and solitude.

Heavens, what had he come to, actually considering working on a Saturday?

Millie emerged from the kitchen, her head wrapped in a red checkered scarf, and deposited a stack of newspapers on the floor beside the knickknack shelf. "There you are. Did you find the packing tape yet?"

"On the bed." He sank into his recliner and stared at the black television screen.

His wife crossed the room to stand in front of him. "Heavens, you look positively morose. Are you getting sick?"

Yes, he almost cried. *Sick of this whole business. Of crates and piles and eating off paper plates because you've packed the dishes.*

"I'm fine." He slumped further in his chair.

"Hmm." She placed a cool hand on his forehead. "No fever, except maybe cabin fever. Why don't you walk over to the Manor and see what progress Justin has made on the roof?"

Sunlight streamed through the front window, beckoning Al outside. Yes, perhaps a walk would cheer him up. The weatherman predicted a high of sixty-eight, beautiful weather for late April. "Maybe I will."

"Good. Rufus could use some exercise too."

At the mention of his name, thereby proving that his hearing loss was entirely selective, Rufus trotted in from the kitchen. Al wrinkled his nose.

"Phew. You said you've been following him

around the yard to make sure he doesn't . . ." He shuddered. "You know."

"I have. I promise." She splayed her hands, looking perplexed.

"You stink," he told the dog, who pranced like an idiot, as though he'd been paid a compliment.

"I've got a couple more." He knew without asking what she was referring to. Her efforts to come up with a name for their bed and breakfast had begun to border on obsession. "What about Ashwood?"

"Ash and wood together are as bad as wood and burn."

"Sunset Manor?"

He scrunched his nose. "Sounds like a retirement home. Keep trying."

With a grumble she went for the leash while he got his jacket. "While you're there, you might ask why he and Susan haven't gone out again."

The ludicrous thought elicited a laugh. "I most certainly will not."

"I don't mean you should pry," she hurried to say. "But if the chance arises."

"It won't." He zipped his jacket. "That's their business, not ours."

She stooped to snap the leash on Rufus's collar and continued as if he had not spoken. "They are obviously attracted to each other. I hope they aren't letting that whole business with the kidnapping accusation stand in the way of romance."

"If I were you, I wouldn't meddle in my boss's love life."

Hands on her hips, she gave him a mock-scowl. "Honestly, Albert, you act as if I didn't know enough to be subtle." A thought occurred to her, and a frown creased her brow. "Speaking of subtlety, never mind. Don't say anything. You'd probably bungle the whole conversation."

Torn between offense and relief, Al took the leash and left the house.

The walk to the Updyke place — he refused to call it a Manor — warmed Al to the point that he unzipped his jacket. An enjoyable breeze carried the scents of spring and blew away the pungent odor of the dog that trotted along beside him. Al approached the house with a lighter spirit, pleased to see three pickup trucks lining the long drive. Four men knelt in pairs at opposite ends of the steepest part of the roof, the *tat-tat-tat* of a nail gun rising from their work. Another two worked on the ground carrying bundles of shingles from a truck bed and tossing them on the ground near an extension ladder.

At their approach, one of the workers

broke away and headed toward them. Al recognized Justin.

"Hey, Mr. Richardson. Stop by to make sure we're earning our paychecks?" The comment was delivered good-naturedly and accompanied by a firm handshake.

"You're making good progress." Al nodded toward a newly roofed section. The onyx laminate was a good choice. The black was attractive against the white siding, and the neat, even rows put him at ease.

"We're on schedule. The hardest part is getting those old slate shingles off. They're a bear to remove, especially with the slope. Oh, and we finished the back awning yesterday. Want to take a look?"

"Sure."

They headed toward the back, rounding a row of overgrown lilac bushes that had bloomed since the last time Al visited. The intoxicating aroma filled his senses, and he noted with pleasure that the blossoms were a combination of deep purple, delicate lavender, and white. They needed pruning, of course, but with a bit of attention they would be glorious.

They surprised a swarm of squirrels. Al dropped Rufus's leash and looked on approvingly as the dog raced after them, barking like a fiend.

"These support columns aren't as bad as I thought." Justin slapped the nearest post with a solid thud. "I was afraid I'd have to shore them up before we did any work up there, but they're sturdy. Some sanding and paint, and they'll be good as new."

"That's one piece of good news, anyway. Something that *doesn't* have to be repaired." Al tried not to look sour, but apparently failed because Justin laughed.

"Feeling the pinch already?"

Al scowled. "When the realtor called this a fixer-upper, she was being kind."

Rufus bounded back to them with something in his mouth.

"What have you found, pup?" Justin squatted on his haunches and took the object from between the dog's teeth. It was a tennis ball, old and dirt-covered, but still inflated. "Do you play fetch?"

Rufus pranced in place, eyes fixed on the ball.

"Okay, then." Justin stood and cocked his arm. "Go get it."

The ball soared long and high, Rufus in hot pursuit. It bounced once before the hound reached it, but then he leaped and snagged it midair before it touched the ground a second time.

Impressed, Al gave a low whistle. "I've

never seen him move like that."

"You didn't train him?"

Al shook his head as Rufus raced back to them, dropped the ball at Justin's feet, and then took a backward step, tail pummeling the air. "He was dropped off at the animal clinic a few years ago. Millie took pity on him and brought him home. I've never played ball with him," he added, a little guiltily.

Justin threw it again, and Rufus leaped even higher, his body twisting like a gymnast's. Al couldn't be sure, but it looked like he was showing off.

On the third throw, Justin asked casually, "Speaking of the clinic, how is Susan?"

Noting the man's nonchalant manner, Al kept his eye on the dog. "Fine, I guess." He cast about for something to add. This sort of thing was his wife's forte, not his. "Millie did mention that she enjoyed the motorcycle ride the other day."

"Did she?" His glance rested on Al a moment before returning to Rufus. "Good to know. Wonder why she hasn't returned my calls."

Sympathy for the younger man stirred Al to offer an excuse. "Business has picked up at the clinic, according to Millie. Maybe she hasn't had a chance."

Justin considered that, and then nodded, his expression one of mild relief. He turned a grateful smile toward Al.

A furious fit of barking erupted in the yard. Al looked up in time to see a green and gray blur leap from the ground toward a tree, a snarling Rufus in hot pursuit. The squirrel landed three feet up the tree trunk, tennis ball tucked beneath its chin like a green goiter, and scampered to the lowest branch. There it stopped, peering down at the indignant dog, who threw back his head and howled his fury.

"Wow." Justin shook his head. "Never saw a squirrel do that before."

"Maybe we ought to call the place the Gray Squirrel Inn," Al muttered.

With some trepidation, Al decided to drop by Cardwell's instead of facing the disorder that had descended on his once-peaceful home. Rufus, thoroughly defeated by the trouncing he'd received from the squirrel, trailed behind with a doleful expression. Even the sight of Bill's Labrador and Fred's German shepherd waiting on the sidewalk outside the drugstore failed to cheer him. Al actually felt a little sorry for the miserable canine. He secured the leash at the hitching post and spared the dog a sympathetic pat on the head.

"Perk up, boy. We'll get them eventually."

Rufus slumped to the sidewalk and rested his head on his paws, apparently unconvinced.

Bells jingled when Al entered, and a half-dozen pairs of eyes fixed on him. A quick scan failed to reveal the one person he'd feared seeing. Thank the good Lord Thacker was not in evidence. Nor, he realized, were Norman and Woody. The knots in his stomach unwound as he selected an empty stool.

He nodded a greeting toward Bill and Fred, and then told Lucy, "Coffee, light. With honey."

Her lips pursed. "A little late for caffeine, don't you think? You know how it affects you."

With a quick glance at the clock, he had to admit her comment was justified. Almost three thirty. He'd spent more time at the Updyke place than he'd realized. Staring into Lucy's disapproving frown, he almost insisted that he was a grown man and could therefore enjoy a cup of coffee whenever he wanted. But the unpleasant prospect of a sleepless night won out. Not to mention the fact that she would probably text Millie, who would veto his request.

Meekly he asked, "Got any decaf?"

His reward was an approving smile. "I'll make a fresh pot just for you." She refilled Fred's iced tea and turned away to do it.

"Quiet day," commented Bill. "Not like last week."

"Thank goodness." Fred dumped a packet of sweetener into his tea and stirred with a straw, ice clinking against the glass. "Surprised me when you joined the fray, Al. Didn't see that coming."

Al regarded the man. Did his neighbors consider him weak? Unwilling to stand up for what he believed? "What's that supposed to mean?"

Fred answered in a hurry. "Nothing bad. Just surprised me, is all. I mean, you haven't said a word one way or another since this thing started. Not that I've heard, anyway."

"I took my time deciding," he replied with dignity.

Beyond Fred, Bill sliced off a piece of pie and speared it with a fork. "I s'pose since you hired an out-of-towner to handle your repairs, it makes sense you'd side with the Council."

Al twisted on the stool to face him fully. "That's part of it." *Not that it's anybody's business who I hire.* "But the more I thought about it, the more I realized this town is failing. As a resident and a future business owner, it's in my best interest if Goose Creek thrives. It's in all our best interests. We're inbred. We need to open our minds to outside ideas, and that means opening our wallets to outside business."

Lucy applauded, and Al, feeling rather proud, sat taller on his stool. In the past few weeks he'd been so intent on not taking sides that he had not articulated his feelings on the matter, even to himself. Fred's expression remained guarded, but Bill looked thoughtful, and he even gave a slow nod.

The door opened, bells chiming, and Miles breezed in. " 'Lo, boys." He mounted an empty stool. "Heard the news?"

Lucy set a coffee mug in front of Al. "What news is that?"

"The Council's made their decision."

Everyone turned toward him. Al swiveled his way. "And? Who'd they pick?"

Miles shrugged. "Dunno. I just saw Jerry hanging a notice on the doors of City Hall. There's gonna be a special town meeting on Thursday in the elementary school gymnasium to announce the Council's decision."

"The elementary school, huh?" Lucy set a bottle of nondairy creamer and a bear-shaped honey container in front of Al.

"They must be expecting a crowd. I hope everybody keeps a level head this time."

Al poured a generous helping of creamer into his cup, turning the dark liquid a milky brown. By everybody, she could only mean one person. But when had Norman ever kept a level head about anything?

Susan stabbed the remote control toward the television and the screen went black. Golf. Yuck. How she dreaded Sunday afternoons. She should have accepted Millie and Al's invitation to lunch after visiting their church this morning, but she didn't want to inflict her sour mood on the cheerful receptionist.

A stack of file folders hovered in her peripheral vision, calling to her from the dinette table. She should continue her review of patient charts.

She eyed Puff, who was sunning himself on a rock beneath the warming light in his aquarium. "All I ever do is paperwork. In school it was textbooks. Now it's charts or financial records."

The bearded dragon cracked open an eye, and then closed it again.

A rumble outside drew her attention. She jerked upright. The familiar sound grew louder until it sounded like it was right outside. Leaping off the couch, she raced to the front window as a motorcycle, black paint and chrome gleaming in the April sunlight, pulled into the driveway below her. Justin. Breath caught in her chest, she watched as he lowered the kickstand and dismounted. When he took off his helmet and grinned up in her direction, her heart thudded against her ribcage.

He'd left four voicemails since Tuesday, and five texts. Though she agonized over the decision, she ignored them all. Daddy was absolutely right. A distraction at this critical time could prove disastrous for her fledgling business.

Below, Justin reached down and unhooked the second helmet — *her* helmet — and lifted it toward her in an unspoken invitation. Biting a finger, she glanced behind her at the stack of folders.

They'll still be here tonight.

But the sun would not. Budding trees and foals frolicking across gentle swells of Kentucky pastures called to her. What was she doing inside when she could be out enjoying the day, her arms wrapped around Justin's waist?

With a grin and a nod, she let the curtain fall closed and raced toward her closet for her sturdiest pair of boots.

CHAPTER NINETEEN

Jerry bounced a pencil eraser absently on the polished surface of his desk and spoke into the phone. "You'll hear about it on Thursday, Fred, along with everyone else."

"We've been friends for a long time. Heck, I even campaigned for you. Can't you give me a hint?"

Everyone in town seemed to be his friend today. Judging by the number of phone calls he'd taken since he arrived at the office this morning, Thursday's town hall meeting would break attendance records. Jerry flipped the pencil over to scribble a note on his to-do list. *Borrow folding chairs from high school.*

"It's just that Wilma's been nagging me to death to call you." Fred's voice held a note of apology.

If Wilma Rightmier got wind of the Council's decision regarding the water tower paint job, three-quarters of the female population of Goose Creek would know it by noon. Of course, that meant they could dispense with the meeting. Rely on the gossip chain to spread the news.

Tempting, but kind of cowardly.

"Sorry, Fred. No can do." The door opened and Sally stepped into his office holding a sheet of paper. Thankful for an excuse to end yet another awkward call, Jerry said quickly, "Listen, I've got to run. See you Thursday."

He punched the button to disconnect before Fred could speak and dropped the receiver into its cradle. "It's not even lunchtime, and that's the eighth call I've had this morning."

Sally shook her head, her smile sympathetic. "I'm getting the calls too. Where were all these friends when I broke my ankle last year?"

The chair squeaked as he tossed the pencil on the desk and rocked back. "Can't tell you how glad I'll be when this is over. Thursday can't get here soon enough for me."

"You might not think so when you see this."

She set the paper on his desk. The heading read PUBLIC DEMONSTRATION PERMIT. Cramped handwriting filled the blanks, and a familiar signature scrawled across the bottom. Norman Pilkington Sr.

A groan rose from the pit of his sinking stomach. "Not again."

"He just left, looking extremely pleased with himself." Sally shook her head. "Diane and Phyllis are going to be hysterical."

"My *wife* is going to be hysterical." Jerry dug at his eyes with a thumb and forefinger.

"I don't suppose you can get a substitute secretary to take the minutes?"

He scowled up at her. "That depends. Can you get a substitute mayor?"

They shared a laugh, and then Jerry rocked forward to reach for the phone. "I'd better call Sheriff Grimes. He'll have to rally the troops for Thursday." The memory of the brick resurfaced. "I think I'll ask if he can have his deputies do some extra patrolling in Goose Creek between now and then. Especially around the Council members' homes."

"Except for a few extra pounds, Rufus is healthy."

Millie stood beside Susan in the reception area, watching the smelly beagle munch happily on a dog cookie. "So why does he" — she gulped back a queasy wave — "eat poop?"

"Any number of reasons. Some dogs do it out of stress or guilt. If he was scolded when he had accidents in the house, he could be trying to hide it." She picked up a paper and handed it to Millie. "I've printed off some common reasons, and suggestions on correcting the behavior. But I have to warn you, fixing the coprophagia may not change the way he smells."

"Surely it will help."

"Every dog has its own unique odor." The girl looked apologetic. "I hate to say it, but maybe Rufus just stinks."

Her pocket beeped, and she extracted her cell phone. Millie noted the appearance of two spots of color on her cheeks as she read the screen.

"Anything important?" Nosy, but only one thing could bring that particular smile to a young woman's lips.

"It's from Justin." Her voice held a happy tone that matched the flush riding high on her face. "We're having dinner tonight, and he says it's okay to wear sandals since he's in his truck today."

"Well thank goodness for that," Millie commented.

"Oh, I don't know. I don't mind the motorcycle." Her gaze turned shy. "In fact, I like it."

With an effort, Millie contained her glee at the unspoken admission. Young love was so much fun to watch.

The door opened. She looked up, expecting their next patient. Instead, a couple entered. Tanned, grinning, and wearing matching mouse ears on their heads.

Doc stepped inside, threw his arms wide, and announced, "We're home!"

"Well, sort of." Lizzie swept across the room and handed both Susan and Millie a small package. "We brought you a souvenir."

Millie opened the bag and pulled out a snow globe. Inside were two black dots, a miniature top hat, and a tiny orange carrot floating in water. The base read *Florida Snowman.*

"How sweet." Susan held hers up and shook it. "Thank you."

Vowing to find a deep drawer for hers, Millie also thanked the grinning couple and tried not to clench her teeth when Lizzie moved the pen cup out of reach.

"How are things going here?" Doc's gaze swept the empty waiting room.

"Picking up," Millie assured him.

Susan nodded. "Things were kind of rough at first, but I think we hit a turning point last week."

"Fine, fine." He rubbed his hands together. "That makes our news easier."

Millie had seen it coming a week ago. "You're not coming back."

Lizzie split into a jaw-breaking grin. "That's right! We bought a villa in Orlando and we're moving next week."

Doc had the grace to look slightly more sympathetic. "Since you're getting your feet under you, there's really no reason for us to stick around. In fact, you'll do better without me hovering over you."

To her credit, Susan controlled her reaction admirably. She agreed with a smile that only trembled a little and congratulated the Forsythes on their retirement. Millie hugged them both and promised to stop by the house to wish them farewell before the end of the week. When they left with Ajax, she and Susan stared at each other in silence.

"I think he's right," Millie eventually offered. "If people know Doc is around, they might not be as eager to accept a new veterinarian."

"I guess so."

"And you are doing a great job by contacting the former patients." Millie tapped the appointment chart. "We've gotten three appointments from those phone calls."

"That's true."

Susan's pocket beeped again, and the worried creases on her forehead cleared. The pretty blush returned as she read the text. Millie had to bite her tongue to keep from asking what Justin said this time. Instead she moved the pen cup back up onto the counter.

The door opened again. Had Doc forgotten something? Instead, a man she did not know stepped inside. Tall, broad-shouldered, a smattering of silver in his military-short hair. And no pet.

"Daddy!" Shock rode high in Susan's tone. "What are you doing here?"

Millie studied the man. Strong, square jaw, thin lips that looked like they rarely saw a smile. She detected a slight resemblance in the shape of the eyes, but Susan apparently took after her mother.

He opened his arms wide. "Don't I get a hug?"

Susan crossed the room for an embrace. A little wooden, in Millie's opinion.

Releasing his daughter, he extended a hand toward Millie. "Tom Jeffries. You must be Mrs. Richardson. Susan told me how helpful you've been during the transition."

She hid a wince at the force of his grip. "Call me Millie. I'm happy to help. You have a wonderful daughter."

His chest swelled. "Yes, I do."

"So, what *are* you doing here, Daddy?" Susan voiced the question tentatively.

All trace of geniality cleared from his face. "After our phone call last night, I decided we should talk in person. You obviously need some levelheaded guidance, so I've cleared my calendar for a few days."

The poor girl's face drained of color. "A few . . . days?"

"I can stay the week if necessary. Nothing takes priority over my little girl." He studied her through narrowed eyes. "That's not a problem, is it?"

Susan's hand slipped into her pocket. A struggle plain on her face, the fabric of her lab coat bulged as she clenched her phone in her fist. But she answered in a voice completely void of emotion. "Of course not. I have no plans."

Millie's heart twisted.

The three o'clock appointment arrived then, a shepherd mix who'd tangled with a raccoon and had a gash in his ear to show for it. Susan ushered the owner and her patient into the back.

Alone with Tom Jeffries, Millie fought a silent battle with herself. She *should* keep her mouth shut. Albert would say Susan's life was none of her business, and he'd be right. But the poor girl had no mother, and clearly the man in front of her was in need of feminine guidance.

She assumed her best maternal smile. "I hope you won't think me impertinent, but I wonder if I could have a word with you about Susan."

"Of course. I'm always happy to talk about my daughter."

"I know I've only just met her, but I've grown quite fond of her in the past few weeks, which is the only reason I feel able to talk to you about this."

He rested his folded hands on the reception desk. "Go ahead."

"Susan obviously has a great deal of respect for you and relies heavily on your guidance."

"I'm fortunate to have a daughter who isn't impulsive, as some young people her age are prone to be." He dipped his head. "She's levelheaded enough to know when she needs someone with more experience."

Millie chose her words carefully. "I wonder if she might be a bit too dependent on your experience."

The pleasant expression chilled. "I'm not sure I follow you."

"It's just that she seems unsure of herself. Her instincts and ideas are good, but when it comes to acting on them, she's unable to make a decision on her own." She drew a breath. "About her business, and her personal life too."

The eyes that bore into hers became rock-hard. "Is this about that construction worker?"

She'd touched a nerve, obviously. "Justin is a responsible young man, a business owner."

"He drives a *motorcycle.*" The last word came out as a snarl.

"A very nice one. A collector's item, I'm told." Never in a million years did Millie think she'd be put in the position of defending a motorcycle, but the man's obvious disdain made her want to stand on the opposite side of the fence. *Any* fence.

"There is no place in Susan's future for a biker in a hardhat. She's worked too hard to throw it away on someone with an unstable profession."

"Unstable?"

"Construction is seasonal and highly dependent upon the economy. She'll be much better off marrying an executive in the private sector, or a surgeon, or an engineer. And not just financially. She needs someone who is her intellectual equal."

"Surely you're not questioning Justin's

intelligence before you've even met him."

He shrugged. "It doesn't take a high I.Q. to nail two pieces of wood together."

At first she thought a phone was buzzing. Then she realized the sound was the buzz of her blood pressure rising. The sheer snobbery of the man rendered her speechless.

"Look, Mrs. Richardson. Millie. I know you're trying to be helpful, but believe me when I say I know my daughter better than anyone else in the world. I have her best interest at heart, and I refuse to stand by and watch her endanger everything she's worked for."

If his expression were any more condescending, she'd be tempted to slap it off. In fact, her palm itched to connect with his face. If she weren't a Christian woman, she'd do it just for the satisfaction of seeing that smirk replaced by her handprint.

"In fact, I'm considering a change so I'll be closer. My bank has a branch in Lexington, and I might be able to pull a few strings to get an expansion. They need an executive on site in central Kentucky."

So he could breathe down her neck. Pity washed over Millie for the poor young woman.

"I can't tell you how relieved I am, knowing Susan has friends who care enough to speak on her behalf. But rest assured, I won't let her go astray." With a glance at his watch, he turned. "I think I'll run over to Lexington and check into my hotel. Would you tell Susan I'll be back at six to take her to dinner?"

Robbed of her voice by a helpless numbness, Millie nodded.

"Thank you. I'm sure I'll be seeing you."

Try as she might, she couldn't help but regard his parting comment as a threat.

A text. She'd ended their relationship with a text.

Susan rolled over on the futon, twisting the blanket into a knot, and covered her head with a pillow. But no matter how hard she pressed against her ears, she couldn't shut out her thoughts.

Coward.

Heartless, spineless jellyfish.

He deserved a phone call at the very least.

But it wasn't a matter of what Justin deserved. It was a matter of what she'd been capable of doing. And she knew without question that she would burst into tears the minute she heard his voice.

Daddy is right. I know he is.

But here, in her dark apartment with Puff

as her only companion, it wasn't a matter of right or wrong. It was a matter of the heart, and hers ached in her chest.

The familiar *beep beep* of an arriving text pierced the silence like an arrow through an apple. Tossing the pillow aside, she scrambled across the mattress on hands and knees to grab at the phone. When she saw the sender was Justin, her fingers trembled so badly she could barely read the screen.

Trying to understand. Failing miserably. I miss you.

The words blurred as tears filled her eyes. For a moment she sat still, head bowed over the phone. Then she wiped her face on the corner of her blanket and returned the phone to the end table.

Why did doing the right thing hurt so much?

CHAPTER TWENTY

An ancient brick building that looked to Al like a detention center housed Goose Creek Elementary School. All three of his children had attended kindergarten through fifth grade here. In all the years he'd lived in Goose Creek, he had never seen the school so crowded.

"I'm glad we walked," Millie said as they turned the corner.

She might as well have said *I told you so,* since he'd wanted to drive. Turns out she was right, but he clamped his teeth against the admission. Parked cars lined the street, and a stream of slow-moving traffic crept along looking for a place to squeeze in.

A crowd had gathered on the sidewalk in front of the school, dozens of signs identifying them as Norman's protest group. Their number seemed to have doubled.

Al nodded in their direction. "He's gaining support."

"I think that's both sides. There's Pete."

Al looked more closely. The throng was comprised of two distinct crews marching along the sidewalk toward each other. Pete's blond head was clearly identifiable among the throng. The sign he carried tonight looked more professionally constructed, with a sturdy wooden post and stenciled lettering that identified him as a Council supporter.

Millie scanned the area. "I'm surprised Franklin and Lulu aren't here. They certainly enjoyed the demonstration last week."

"I didn't tell him about it."

Al felt no guilt at the admission. Pete had called earlier in the week to try to enlist him in tonight's demonstration, which he politely declined. Now that he had publicly thrown his hat into the ring as a Council supporter, he would stand by his decision, but joining a protest march was entirely out of the question. Thacker, on the other hand, would have leaped in with enthusiasm, which is why Al purposefully kept the information from his coworker. In just over a week, the Thackers would officially become Creekers. After that he would have no way of escaping the man. He saw absolutely nothing wrong in preserving his privacy in the meantime.

As Al and Millie neared the building, Norman and Pete approached each other. Tension rode high among protesters and onlookers alike as the two exchanged glares.

"Oh, dear." Millie's hand tightened on his arm. "I hope they keep their heads about them."

"If they don't, they won't be here long enough to hear the announcement." Al pointed out a line of uniformed officers standing near the front doors of the schoolhouse, watching the confrontation.

When a scant three yards lay between the two leaders, they halted. Glares were exchanged. There may have been mutters, which Al couldn't hear at this distance. At the same moment the two whirled and retreated, marching in the direction they'd just come. The Richardsons joined the rest of the onlookers in breathing a sigh of relief.

"Look, there's Violet."

Their stout neighbor caught sight of them and hurried over. "We're gonna be packed like sardines in that gymnasium," she announced. "Squashed like zucchini. Elbow to elbow, shoulder to shoulder."

Millie tossed him a warning glance and replied before he could roll his eyes. "We'd better get inside, then. I want to get a seat."

Rather than cross the picket line, Al made

his way through the grass. He nodded a greeting at the stern-faced deputies, who did not respond, and joined a slow-moving stream of Creekers entering the building. The familiar smell of pencil erasers and old books permeated the air, reminding him of PTA meetings when the kids were younger.

Folding metal chairs crowded the gymnasium floor, row upon row of them, set up to face the stage at the far end beneath the basketball goal. Most were occupied, though the first few rows on each side of the center aisle had been roped off. The bleachers had been pulled out along one side, and they were less crowded.

"There's Susan," Millie announced, her voice relieved. She took off toward the bleachers, Violet in tow.

Al opened his mouth to protest. He didn't relish the prospect of sitting on a hard bench with nothing to lean against, but his wife plunged into the crowd. Unless he wanted to sit alone, he had no choice but to follow.

The veterinarian greeted them with a polite smile that failed to reach her eyes. Millie had told him about her father's arrival and her subsequent dumping of Hinkle. Looking at her tonight, she certainly didn't look happy about it. In fact, she looked downright miserable.

"I'm glad you came," Millie told the girl when they'd settled themselves beside her.

"The more I thought about it, I realized you were right. Since I'm a new resident, I'd better put in an appearance."

Violet leaned forward and spoke over Al. "A Creeker, dear. That's what we call ourselves."

Susan nodded, her expression serious. "Creeker. I'll remember."

"And where's your father?" Al glanced around the area, looking for a tyrant with an unkind gleam in his eye. According to Millie, the man might well have horns on his head.

"I forgot to tell you. He got called back to Paducah for an urgent meeting." Millie offered the explanation in a distracted manner, busily scanning the gymnasium.

"He'll be back up for the weekend to go over the clinic's books," Susan offered. "Accounting isn't one of my strong points, but it definitely is his."

Her reply held neither sorrow nor relief, which stirred a sympathetic response in Al. Millie was right. The poor girl was being suffocated by her well-intentioned father, and she didn't even realize it. Millie interrupted her perusal of the crowd to flash him a knowing glance, and then returned her attention to searching the attendees. No doubt taking mental notes of who attended and who didn't so she could compare notes with her cronies tomorrow.

A commotion on the floor drew Al's attention. Norman and his followers filed through the door, led by a pair of deputies. They marched down the center aisle, signs held high. Little Norm had even donned fresh jeans, a collared shirt, and a tie, at which he plucked continually. Their guide led them to the reserved seats in the front.

"Is the mayor crazy, sitting them up front like that?" Al asked Millie.

When Norman's group had been seated, another pair of deputies led the opposition into the gym. They took their seats with many a glare exchanged across the aisle.

Finally, Mayor Jerry Selbo entered from the left side of the stage. A loud hiss erupted from the crowd and rose as everyone shushed everyone else. The mayor crossed to a metal music stand in the center of the dais and tapped a microphone beside it. The minor explosions amplified through the speakers, and the crowd settled.

"Thanks, everyone, for coming out tonight."

A screech of feedback pierced the air, and

most of the audience slapped hands over their ears. A technician raced onto the stage toward a control box, and the feedback ceased. The man straightened and pointed toward Jerry.

"Sorry about that." The mayor gave an apologetic shrug. "Anyway, as I was saying, the format of tonight's town meeting will be a bit different, since some of the Council members felt it was in their best interest not to attend."

Al scanned the crowd and spotted Lynn Bowers' red head, flanked by Gary Vandergrift and Aaron Southworth. Beside Gary, Sally held a pen poised above a notepad. He saw no sign of Diane or Phyllis.

Jerry continued. "Personally, I think it's a shame when an elected official feels threatened to appear in public. And their fears are not unfounded. I'm sure it will come as a surprise to most of you that we have received threats and been the victims of vandalism over the issue of the painting of the water tower." A murmur raced through the auditorium. "These acts are uncharacteristic of the good people of Goose Creek, and frankly, they sadden me."

His expressive face did look sad, almost stricken, like a father who has learned of his child's grievous misbehavior. Al scanned the assemblage. Most of the audience displayed surprise, though a few hung their heads guiltily.

Now Jerry straightened, his expression confident. "Tonight I trust we can put our differences behind us. In just a moment I will announce the name of the individual who has been awarded the job of painting the Goose Creek water tower. The Council received eight bids for the job."

Eight? Al exchanged a surprised glance with Millie. He'd no idea there would be so much interest.

"Each one was prepared with professionalism and attention to detail." Jerry's gaze focused on Little Norm in the front row, and he nodded an acknowledgement. "The Council discussed them all at length. In fact, it was the longest Council meeting on record. I'm not exaggerating when I say we agonized over our decision. But in the end, the vote was unanimous."

He halted. An expectant hush settled over the audience. Al found that his palms were damp, and he wiped them on his slacks.

"The job of painting the Goose Creek water tower will be done by" — a final pause — "Ms. Sandra Barnes of Atlanta, Georgia."

Pandemonium erupted. Pete's group

broke into applause, whooping their victory and waving their signs high in the air. On the opposite side of the floor, Norman leaped to his feet. His shouts of, "No fair! No fair!" were augmented by Hazel's cry to, "Impeach the mayor! Impeach the whole Council!" The deputies, stationed strategically at either side of the stage, moved to form a protective line between the front row and the stage, where Jerry stood calmly, hands clasped in front of him, waiting for the uproar to die down.

Al shifted on the hard bench. He'd expected this, of course. But now that the job had been awarded to an outsider, he couldn't help but worry about the repercussions. And a woman! No doubt that would add fuel to the discontent among chauvinistic old timers, of which there were more than a few. Would Saturdays at Cardwell's ever be the same?

When the clamor had calmed enough for him to be heard, Jerry spoke again.

"I've had several long conversations with Ms. Barnes, and she's well aware of the controversy this issue has caused. Though I advised against it, she insisted on being here tonight. She wanted an opportunity to meet you and to show you a sample of her work." His expression became stern, and he swept the gymnasium from one end to the other, spending an extra-long time staring at Norman. "I know the residents of Goose Creek will treat her with the respect and hospitality a lady visitor deserves. So please join me in welcoming Ms. Sandra Barnes."

Looking toward the side stage, he stepped back from the microphone and began to applaud. Al joined, as did most everyone else. Norman, he noticed, sat stubbornly with his arms folded tightly across his chest.

Two people emerged from stage left to join the mayor. One was Sheriff Grimes, whose presence made a statement that needed no interpretation. The woman beside him walked with a sure step, long-legged enough to keep pace with him. She stood nearly as tall as Grimes, who wasn't a small man. Big boned and sturdy, she wore jeans, a belt with a gigantic turquoise buckle, and a worn leather vest over a starchy white shirt. Her boot heels clomped solidly across the stage. Her hair hung halfway down her back in a long, straight braid. Al recognized her immediately as the woman he'd seen a week or so ago drinking coffee at Cardwell's.

Millie leaned over to whisper. "She looks like a Texan to me."

Behind her, the same technician who'd

fixed the sound system wheeled out a rolling cart with a projector mounted on it and positioned it beside the music stand. He stretched an extension cord to the back of the stage and pulled down a portable video screen.

The sheriff stood to one side beside the mayor while Ms. Barnes approached the microphone.

"First I'd like to thank y'all for trusting me with such an important job." Her voice drawled, betraying a deep Southern influence. "Mayor Selbo's told me about all the trouble you've been having, and I want you to know I understand. It's not my place to comment on the right or the wrong of the decision. All I can do is express my thanks and pledge to you that you won't be sorry you hired me."

An impressive opening statement. Al found himself approving of this woman's approach.

"Now, I'm not much for speeches, so I'll make this quick. I'm not just a painter. I consider myself an artist. It just so happens I'm not all that fond of canvas or paper." She grinned. "I'm originally from Texas, so I like to do things in a big way."

Millie caught Al's eye and nodded.

Ms. Barnes pressed a button on the projector the technician had set up, and the screen behind her displayed an image. Somewhere someone flipped a light switch, and half the lights in the gym went out so everyone could get a better view.

The picture was of a billboard depicting a cowboy with an infectious grin, his hat pushed back on his forehead. The fancy lettering read *Welcome to Lawry, Wyoming*. An impressed murmur rose from the onlookers.

"This was one of my first commercial jobs," Ms. Barnes explained. "People aren't my favorite subjects, but this guy happened to be the son of one of the town's most prominent residents. I thought he was mighty fine to look at."

The comment was met with feminine laughter. Beside Al, Violet tittered and fanned her face.

The picture changed. A concrete wall had been covered in a colorful mosaic of artistic designs, the overall impression fascinating and appealing. "This is the side of a building in the Bronx, and a while back it was a favorite target for graffiti. Some of the stuff spray painted on there was, well, let's just say, objectionable. They hired me to do something that teenagers wouldn't want to cover up." She glanced toward her audience with a satisfied nod. "It worked."

The next photo appeared and was met with an audible gasp. A water tower, the barrel rounder and wider than theirs, had been painted to resemble a city block. Skyscrapers rose into the night, windows aglow. Cars lined the street, and pedestrians dressed in overcoats hurried past shops.

"This one is on the outskirts of Chicago." She cocked her head and pointed. "See that blue Honda there? That's my mother's car. She wanted to be in one of my paintings, and I've learned it's always best to keep my momma happy. If you look real close, you'll see her behind the wheel."

She turned back to face the audience, who had fallen silent as they gazed at the painting. Even Norman, Al noticed, had sunk down in his chair.

"When I saw the RFB for your water tower, I was immediately drawn to the job because of the name of your town. Goose Creek, Kentucky." She smiled. "It sounds like such a quaint, friendly place."

Though no one made a sound, a wave of almost palpable shame swept through the gymnasium. Al felt his share as well. He certainly hadn't acted any friendlier than the rest of the Creekers in the past few weeks.

"I even got in my car and zipped up here the next day. Drove through the town, took some pictures, had a cup of coffee at the soda fountain in Cardwell Drugstore." A smattering of applause answered her. She planted a hand on her hip. "You know what y'all need, though? A motel or an inn or something. I had to stay overnight in Lexington."

Millie turned a triumphant grin his way. He patted her on the leg and directed his attention to Ms. Barnes.

"Anyway, I went back home and came up with a sketch that I think fits this place. I included it in the bid I sent to the mayor, and I think that's one reason he hired me." She grew serious. "I'm going to show it to you, but I want you to know it's rough. Something I threw together. The final will be a lot better." Her chest expanded as she drew a slow, deep breath. "So here it is."

She pressed a button, and the image changed. Al studied it, and a feeling of immense satisfaction blossomed in him. She had drawn their water tower, though flattened like a map of the earth to depict all sides. Across the surface lay a lush, peaceful valley, green rolling hills outlined by a sprawling fence that resembled the one around the park at the edge of town. Blue-green water rushed across a rocky creek bed, so realistic Al could almost hear the peaceful babble. Overhead, a flock of geese flew in a V formation, their feathers capturing the sunlight. The words *Goose Creek, Kentucky* swept across the sky above them.

The letters, Al noted with immense satisfaction, were perfectly straight.

An awed silence stretched on as people examined the artwork. Finally, it was broken by the sound of a single person's applause.

On the front row, Little Norm Pilkington stood from his chair, clapping with enthusiasm.

Within seconds, he was joined by nearly everyone in the place. Mayor Selbo folded his arms across his chest and gave a nod, his satisfied gaze sweeping over his constituents. Behind the podium, Ms. Barnes flashed a Texas-sized grin as the people of Goose Creek gave her their thunderous approval.

Susan stood outside on the front lawn of the school building, her arm captured in Millie's grip. Her attempts to tug free and head for home had been firmly resisted. The sweet little receptionist could be downright stubborn when she put her mind to it. Her husband stood to one side, hands clasped behind his back, looking patiently bored.

"Really, dear, you should join us at Cardwell's. Everyone will be there." Millie spoke without looking at her. Instead, she constantly studied the faces streaming past them. "You need to establish a presence in town. Let people become accustomed to seeing you."

"I'm sure you're right." Susan attempted, gently, to separate herself, to no avail. "But I'm not feeling very sociable tonight. I really just want to go home and get a good night's sleep."

She could hope, anyway. She hadn't slept well since Tuesday.

"But this is a golden opportunity. We hardly ever have so many people out at one time."

Susan was saved from replying by Millie's friend Violet, who arrived slightly out of breath.

"You'll never believe what just happened. Everybody was crowding around Ms. Barnes, congratulating her and wanting to shake her hand. Little Norm pushed his way through them, marched right up to her and offered to be her assistant *for free.* Said he wants to learn her technique." A wicked gleam flashed in her eyes. "Norman stood beside him, squirming like a slug in salt."

"Good for Little Norm," Millie replied. "It's about time that young man stood up to his father." She shot a quick glance at Susan, who felt herself beginning to bristle. Was that comment aimed at her?

Before she could formulate a reply, Millie's eyes widened as she caught sight of something behind her. "Dear, if you really prefer to go home, then of course you must. I'll see you tomorrow." She released Susan's arm to grab hold of Al with one hand and Violet with the other. "Come on, you two. We'd better hurry if we want to get a seat."

With a speed that left Susan's head spinning, she pulled them away. Al's expression betrayed a bewilderment that matched her own as they disappeared into the crowd. Odd woman, that Millie. Nice, but odd. With a shrug, she turned toward the sidewalk —

— and ran straight into Justin.

Several things became clear at once. Millie's insistence that she attend tonight's meeting. Her distracted manner all evening. The firm grip that refused to let her go until *she* was ready, and the sudden dismissal and subsequent speedy retreat.

But those things dissolved as her eyes were captured by Justin's. Her surroundings faded. Voices dimmed and were drowned out by the drumbeat of her pulse.

"Can we talk?"

She ought to say no. Ought to leave now, before he had a chance to say a word. Maybe she did owe him an explanation, but she could text it to him. And yet . . .

Numbly, she nodded.

He glanced around, and then took her hand to pull her away from the crowd. A thrill shot up her arm at the touch of his fingers. Heart in her throat, she allowed him to guide her around the side of the school building where a playground lay in darkness. Wood chips crunched beneath her sneakers as they approached a dome-shaped jungle gym.

When he released her hand, her skin felt cold, bereft of his touch. But she had no time to think about that because once again her eyes were drawn to his, held prisoner in the depths that the night turned black.

"Why?"

One word. But it held an agony of emotion that stirred a response in her. Tears stung her eyes, and she looked away. "I . . . I have a new business."

"So do I." He dipped his head, trying to recapture her eyes. "I just went out on my own last year."

"Then you understand how hard it is. We

have to focus, build our customer base. We don't have time for . . ."

"For what?"

For love. Those were the words that almost crossed her lips.

"For distractions," she said.

He stepped closer. Every nerve in her body tingled with the awareness that Justin stood less than a foot in front of her, and that she ought to retreat. Back up. But her feet refused to cooperate.

"Am I a distraction, Susan?" At the sound of her name spoken in that deep, gravelly voice, her stomach began to flutter.

"Yes," she replied, breathless. Realizing what she said, she shook her head. "I mean, no. Not *you,* per se. Anything that takes my attention away from the business is a distraction."

His hand rose, and he placed a thumb beneath her chin to tilt her head back. How could such a gentle contact, no more than an inch of his skin touching hers, set off such a riot of emotion?

"That doesn't sound like my Susan talking."

"I — He —" She gulped and tried again. "My father is only thinking of me. He's supported me in everything I've ever done. I wouldn't have been able to buy the clinic if it weren't for him. He's all I've got."

"I understand what an important part of your life your father is. I've never met him, but he must be an amazing man to have raised a daughter like you." He moved closer, so close his breath warmed her skin. "But you're wrong. He isn't all you have. You have me." His voice lowered to a raspy whisper. "I think I'm falling in love with you, Susan."

The words rang in her ears, resonated in her soul. An explosion of emotions burst inside her, joy and elation, wonder and awe. *He loves me. And I love him.*

How will I ever get the nerve to tell Daddy?

Thumb still beneath her chin, Justin's fingers spread open and crept up her cheek to cup her face. He leaned toward her, or maybe she leaned toward him. She didn't know and didn't care. The moment their lips touched, a giddy sense of elation transported her to a place she'd only dreamed of. Her questions died, brushed away by Justin's kiss.

Perhaps mustering the nerve to tell Daddy wouldn't be so hard after all.

CHAPTER TWENTY-ONE

On moving day Al awoke to the bedspread being ripped unceremoniously off the bed. Shivering, he opened his eyes to find Millie standing over him with a red bandana tied around her head.

"I've got to get it packed before everyone shows up." She folded the bedspread and placed it in an open cardboard box and then pointed toward the bedside table. "There's your coffee. Your clothes are in the bathroom. Fold your pajamas and leave them on the vanity so I can pack them. Now get up, please, so I can strip the bed."

No cheerful good morning greeting. No pleasant off-key humming as she scrambled his eggs. Just, "Up and at 'em!" like a drill sergeant. The militant Millie had been in evidence more and more in the past week. She barked orders ruthlessly, checking items off her list with a fierce flourish that left him scurrying to do her bidding. Where had his sweet Millie gone? Oh, how he missed her.

Rolling out of bed, he reached for the steaming Styrofoam cup. He missed real dishes, too. And real food. Though he now considered himself a connoisseur of fast food French fries — he preferred the thin, crispy ones that left disturbing grease marks on the napkin — he missed real potatoes whipped with cream and drenched in Millie's country gravy.

Dodging an array of cardboard boxes, he gulped coffee on the way to the bathroom to change clothes as instructed.

Contrary to the weatherman's dire predictions for a soggy Saturday, the sun rose lemony yellow in a cloudless sky. Dressed and downstairs, Al took his bagel — untoasted, since the toaster had been packed away days ago — and a second cup of coffee outside to enjoy his last breakfast on his deck. Correction. Franklin Thacker's deck. The papers had been signed and the money exchanged yesterday.

A loud engine roared into the driveway at the front of the house as he was licking the last bit of cream cheese off his fingers. Millie stuck her head through the door.

"The boys are here with the truck." Their sons, David and Doug, had come down from Cincinnati to help. They'd offered to pick up the U-Haul in Lexington and bring it over this morning.

Al wiped his lips and for a moment considered throwing the napkin in the yard for Thacker to clean up. Instead he wadded it into a ball and, resigned to the day, turned toward his wife.

"All right. I'm coming."

She studied him a moment and then stepped outside, closing the door behind her. An understanding expression softened her features as she crossed the deck and wrapped her arms around him.

"I know it's hard. We've lived a lot of life in this house."

"Yes we have." He returned her embrace, relishing in the resurgence of the tender Millie he loved best.

She laid her head on his shoulder. "I'm sorry to leave it."

"Are you?" Pulling back, he gazed down at her. "You seem so gung-ho about the bed and breakfast."

"I am." She turned in his arms and nestled back against his chest, her head fitting comfortably into the hollow beneath his chin. "But sad too. We're turning the page on an important chapter in our life."

A note of sadness in her voice stirred in

him a protective instinct that had sprung to life thirty-seven years before. He couldn't stand to see his wife, his Millie, sad. As long as he lived, his job was to make her happy.

He tightened his arms around her and rested his cheek against the top of her head. "We're beginning a new chapter. A new adventure. Just you and me."

"And Rufus," she reminded him, a giggle in her voice.

"How could I forget Rufus?"

The door opened and the head of their oldest twin, David, emerged. "There you are. Half the town is here to help. You want to come tell us what goes where?"

Al indulged in one more hug before releasing his wife. She stepped out of his embrace, a transformation occurring in the time it took her to cross the deck door.

"Okay, let's get this done," she commanded at the top of her lungs. "Boxes in the pickups, furniture in the van. Upstairs first."

Smiling, Al followed, prepared to do as he was told.

Inside the house he dodged a dozen people heading upstairs. As David said, it did seem that half the town had showed up to help them move. Chuck, Fred, and Ralph balanced boxes in their arms, while Pete and Woody stood at opposite ends of the sofa, ready to pick it up. Thank goodness those two were on speaking terms again. Nodding his thanks, he picked up a pair of table lamps and strode outside.

More Creekers had gathered on the front lawn, and half a dozen pickups lined the street. Doug and David were lowering the back ramp on the U-Haul. At the end of the walkway, Little Norm stood in the bed of his pickup arranging the boxes that were handed up to him.

"Can't tell you how much we appreciate your help," Al said as he held up the lamps.

The young man waved off his thanks. "That's what Creekers do. We help each other out."

A car pulled into the driveway in front of the U-Haul. When the driver emerged, Al experienced a rush of annoyance. What was Thacker doing here?

Then he remembered. The man *lived* here.

Thacker caught sight of him and rounded the bumper, waving toward the activity that surrounded them. "Now that's what I call a parade."

Al scanned the yard. People streamed out of the house, arms laden with boxes and furniture. They smiled at one another, calling out the occasional joke, laughing and happy. Neighbors, all of them. Even better, friends.

His mood light, he managed to smile at Thacker. "You're right. Quite a parade."

"So, what'd you think of Mrs. R's surprise?"

Al stared at the man. "What surprise?"

Thacker's eyes went wide, and he clapped both hands over his mouth. "Oops. Not a thing, Bert. Not a thing." He looked over Al's shoulder and a frown descended on his face. Cupping his hands around his mouth, he shouted. "Hey, watch out for that bushy thing there. You almost trampled it. And keep to the sidewalk. I don't want my grass smashed to smithereens before I even move in."

Gritting his teeth, Al headed toward the house to retrieve another load.

Though Al would never have thought it possible, by the time the day ended the house on Mulberry Avenue was empty. The Updyke house, on the other hand, was stuffed to the bursting point. Who would have thought that the contents of their twenty-two hundred square foot home would fill a space three times that size? Of course, their furniture had to be squeezed in beside the dusty old stuff the Updykes left behind, which Millie insisted would be perfect for their bed and breakfast when it was cleaned up and refinished.

The horde had deposited the last truck-load and left. Finally, he and Millie were alone. She'd made hot tea and they'd collapsed into their lounge chairs on the back porch, or verandah, as she insisted on calling it. Herbal tea, not that there was any danger of a sleepless night tonight. Exhaustion resonated in every cell of his body. From the way her eyelids drooped as she slumped in the chair beside him, Millie felt the same.

"Quite a turnout today," he commented.

"I lost count," Millie confessed. "I want to send everyone a thank-you note, but I know I'll miss someone." She paused, and then continued with a smile in her voice. "Did you see Susan and Justin kissing in the side yard?"

Al chuckled softly. "The whole town saw them. Not that they noticed. I don't think either of them saw anyone but each other."

She breathed a sigh. "I love happy endings."

He didn't mention it, but he doubted if Mr. Jeffries would let things end there. No doubt there would be more chapters to read in Susan and Justin's story.

"Oh look, Albert." Tiredness dragged at her voice, but she managed to lift a hand and point. "There are geese by the pond."

He examined the small flock of Canada geese. "Nasty things, geese. Leave a mess wherever they go. And they bite. My advice is to steer clear of them."

She punched him on the arm in a playful reprimand. Then she sat up. "Look there. I can't believe how close that squirrel is coming."

Sure enough, one of the dozen or so varmints who frolicked between the trees had decided to venture toward them. Al glanced down at Rufus, waiting for him to notice the approaching intruder. The squirrel scurried a foot or two in their direction, then stopped. It stood upright, eyed the dog, and then dropped down to all fours to edge closer.

"It's coming for his food," Millie whispered.

They'd set Rufus's food and water bowl on the edge of the porch earlier in the day, when they'd had to secure him to the post to keep him from getting underfoot. Though the rope had been untied an hour ago, they hadn't yet picked the bowls up.

The squirrel halted one last time about a yard away. Rufus finally stirred enough to raise his head.

Here it comes. That rodent's about to learn a lesson he won't forget.

Al watched, anticipation mounting. The animals regarded each other. The squirrel inched closer, its body tense, tail twitching, ready to dash away at the first sign of trouble.

Trouble that never came.

Unbelievably, the squirrel covered the last foot without a peep from Rufus. It inspected the contents of the bowl, sniffing with a cautious eye fixed on the dog. Apparently deciding the dry dog food would suit, it shoved chunks into its mouth until both cheeks bulged. Then it turned and retreated at a pace that might be called a victory strut. Rufus let out a sigh and dropped his head onto his paws.

Al regarded the dog with disgust. "Traitor."

Rufus closed his eyes and rolled onto his side, while Millie's laughter rang over the lawn. How could Al not enjoy such a delightful sound?

She settled back in her chair and drained her tea mug. "So what are we going to call this place? How about Richardson Manor?"

He shook his head. "Too plain."

"Millie's Manor?"

He dipped his head and gave her a look out of the top of his eyeballs.

She laughed. "Just kidding. What about the Lantern Inn?"

He glanced around the yard. "We have a lantern?"

"No, but we could buy one."

"It's not in the budget."

Silence descended between them, comfortable and peaceful. He almost hated to intrude with a suggestion, but voiced his idea anyway. "What about keeping it simple? The Goose Creek Bed and Breakfast."

She sat straight up, mouth gaping. For a moment he thought she would veto the idea outright. Then she closed it again, and tilted her head as she considered the suggestion.

"You know, I like it." Settling back in her chair, she smiled. "The Goose Creek Bed and Breakfast. That's a winner."

They fell silent again as the sun dipped below the tree line beyond the pond. The squirrels disappeared as the last rays of light dimmed, deserting the sky to a spreading dark purple night.

"So you haven't said much about my surprise." Millie's voice held a note of disappointment. "Don't you like it?"

Al turned his head toward the side of the house, where the back end of his new/used

Airstream RV was parked. How Millie had convinced Thacker to throw it into the deal, he had no idea. Like the house they'd just bought, it needed a lot of work. He didn't mind. He had three years before retirement, plenty of time to do all the minor repairs it needed.

"I love it. Thank you." He extended his hand sideways and grasped hers. "And I love you."

"I love you too." The fading light caught one of those kissable dimples on her cheek. "If I weren't so tired, I'd prove it."

They shared a laugh, and he squeezed her hand. If there was a luckier man in all of Goose Creek, he couldn't imagine who it would be. He had the best woman in town right here beside him.

Quite the little fixer-upper, his Millie.

ACKNOWLEDGMENTS

The more I write, the more certain I am that I couldn't do my job without the help and support of many people. In creating the fictitious town of Goose Creek and writing stories about the characters who live there, I'm thankful for the assistance of more people than I can easily list here. But it seems churlish not to say thank you, so I'll give it a try.

Thank you to the cities of Midway and Frankfort, Kentucky, for providing the inspiration for the charming, small-town atmosphere I've tried to create in Goose Creek. I love walking your streets, admiring your quaint shops, chatting with your residents, and pausing every so often to see a train plow through the middle of everything.

Thank you to Jerry Selbo for allowing me

to use his name for my fictitious mayor. Jerry won the opportunity to have a character named after him during a fundraising auction at Mountain Vista United Methodist Church, where we worship together. Though the mayor of Goose Creek is fictional, I enjoyed giving him a few of Jerry's characteristics, such as his love for music and his levelheadedness in the face of conflict.

Thank you to my friend Lynn Bowers for answering questions about serving on the City Council, and for graciously allowing me to use her name for my fictitious councilwoman.

Thank you to three very special author friends who helped me craft the story and characters of Goose Creek: Amy Barkman (a.k.a. Mom), Anna Zogg, and Marilynn Rockelman. These ladies are brainstormers extraordinaire!

Thank you to the professional team that makes the Goose Creek Stories possible: my agent, Wendy Lawton; my editor, Kathleen Kerr; and everyone else at Harvest House Publishers for caring about this story and working so hard to make it good.

Thank you to my husband, Ted Smith,

for . . . gosh, for so much! Not only is he the most supportive, encouraging husband a writer could ask for, but he is the inspiration for every romantic heartthrob I've ever written. There's a song that says, "I love how you love me." I do, Ted. For that, and so much more.

Above all thank you to my Lord and Savior, Jesus Christ, the true Author of all stories worth reading.

To learn more about books by Virginia Smith or to read sample chapters, log on to our website:

www.harvesthousepublishers.com

ABOUT THE AUTHOR

Virginia Smith is the author of more than 20 inspirational novels and 50 articles and short stories. An avid reader with eclectic tastes in fiction, Ginny writes in a variety of styles, from lighthearted relationship stories to breath-snatching suspense.

p. 269